DEAD OVER

HEELS FOR

YOU

PERSEPHONE PRINGLE COZY MYSTERIES: FIVE

PATTI LARSEN

Thanks, Kirstin!

ISBN: 978-1-989925-80-5

CHAPTER ONE

Belladonna crouched unhappily inside her carrier, meowing aggressively from the back seat while I did my best to comfort her on the ride to our destination.

"I know you hate it," I told my fluffy white partner in therapy, her anxious scratching at the padded doorway to her so-called prison accompanied by plaintive cries for freedom. "I'm sorry, Bella, I really am. It's for your protection, sweetie." Ever since I'd adopted her, we'd had a love/hate back and forth battle with the roomy and rather expensive carrier I'd purchased for her, Belladonna's joy of riding in the car clearly eliminated with the forced confinement I made her endure. The times I had agreed to let her ride, instead, in the padded pet booster seat I'd bought for her, I'd worried endlessly about what might happen to her if we had an accident. And since she refused—outright refused with the skills of a master thief and escape artist able to undo any buckle or snap—to wear a collar or harness, that meant we fought over the carrier at least once a week.

"Not giving in," I told her as I pulled up to the front of the Briarwood Hotel, grateful the drive was only ten minutes from home because if I was forced to listen to her yowl and meow and whimper much longer, I was going to cave and let her out, despite what I might say out loud. Belladonna rubbed vigorously against the mesh, white fur leaving strands behind in the back seat, her need to escape growing more extravagant as I unbuckled the rugged container from the seatbelt and hefted her out into the warm August morning. "We have a client, miss," I said, the SUV's alarm beeping as I locked it up and headed inside, smiling and nodding, a little embarrassed by my cat's loud and rather petulant protestations when a pair of guests made happy noises over her carrier. "I expect you to behave yourself."

She blinked her giant, green eyes at me, the pupils widening as we passed from the sunlit morning into the dimmer, elegant interior of the old hotel, my sandals clicking softly on the marble floors, the scent of breakfast wafting from the nearby dining room. Reminded me I'd only had time for coffee this morning, that the hasty phone call I'd taken had me on the move quicker than I'd expected.

Not that my old friend and classmate, Dr. Richard Renfrew, was prone to hysteria or anything, but his plea for me to say yes to a new and rather hush-hush client intrigued me enough I immediately responded in the affirmative.

"Your contact will meet you in the lobby," Richard told me, sounding relieved. "Seph, I'm very grateful for this. They asked me to come to Wallace and I planned to, but I had two emergencies and was called to court. I've already filled them in about you and had you in mind when I found out where she'd be."

"Are you going to tell me who it is I'm treating?" Not that it had mattered, since I'd already made up my mind and was on the move while we continued our conversation.

"I can't, Seph," he said. "I'm sorry for the secrecy, but you'll understand when you meet Jane."

"Jane Doe," I said, almost laughing but suppressing it to a mere snort.

"Smith, actually," he said. "Clandestine, I know." Richard chuckled himself. "It's an easy gig, I promise. Just listen to her, that's all. She'll think you're glorious."

She would, would she, this mysterious Jane Smith? Well, I was, though I didn't tell Richard that. He had a big enough ego he might be jealous and change his mind about handing over an important client to an old classmate who outscored him every time.

Snort. Now, who had the ego?

I slowed my forward motion as I neared the wide, dark wooded front desk, the beautifully maintained lobby reminding me of a movie set with the deep brown leather furniture and towering ceiling, sparkling chandeliers in a long row down the center of the space. Which had me guessing, naturally, about who it was I was here to see.

Since Richard lived in Los Angeles, and the fact a film crew moved in a week ago to shoot a romcom tied into knowing the media loved a good star breakdown story, it all made sense. If I was a famous someone in need of therapy, I'd likely have done my best to keep that fact from the prying general public, thus the super-secret meeting I'd been hired for. Still, it all felt a little silly, really. However, if this was what the client needed, so be it.

Belladonna meeped softly, her struggle ceasing for the moment, though the plaintive sound had my guilt rising all over again. I did my best to be as inconspicuous as possible, hard to do with a cat in a carrier, a cat who again began her expression of vocal discontent with renewed vigor as someone walked past. As if a stranger might come to her rescue since I, her human, was such a terrible person.

"Hush, Bella," I said, sighing deeply, now regretting I'd brought her. My suggestion the client come to me had been outright rejected, which meant a house call, but I hadn't *needed* to bring my cat, her therapeutic tendencies and good nature notwithstanding. "Don't make me take you home, young lady."

She settled at last, glaring up at me. I'd suffer for this later, no doubt.

Fortunately, I didn't have long to wait. "Dr. Pringle, I presume?" I looked up from Belladonna's unhappy crouch to find a tall, middle-aged man in a dark suit had come to a halt next to me. He held out one hand, shaking mine as he smiled down at Belladonna's carrier, speaking again before I could correct his use of a title I didn't own. Had Richard told him otherwise or was it a natural mistake? I certainly hoped the latter because while my classmate had finished his Ph.D., this girl had gone on to other things when academia became suffocating. "You have a cat? Excellent." He exhaled a sigh that sounded like relief, gesturing for me to join him as he strode toward the elevators. I followed, stepping on board with him when the doors opened instantly to his summons. "She loves cats. My apologies," he said then, "Thomas Parker."

"Mr. Parker," I said. "While I realize there's a security issue, now that I'm here, a little background might be helpful."

"I'm sorry about the secrecy," he said instantly, smooth voice a pleasant tenor as he checked his phone before sliding it back into the interior pocket of his dress jacket. I shifted my feet on the carpeted floor of the elevator, catching Belladonna's continuing glare in the polished brass doors. "It's a delicate situation and while we understand Dr. Renfrew's prior commitments, it's good to know one of his peers could step in and take on her sessions."

It wasn't hard to figure out who it was I'd come to talk to. Not with Callie working as a PA on set, loving her job so much she told me every last detail when I managed to see her, which wasn't much since they kept her running day and night, it seemed. Her mention of the volatility of one particular member of the cast had me reasonably confident I already knew the identity of this mysterious client.

I was about to respond when Thomas went on, voice dropping, expression now stern.

"I do hope you understand the gravity of this opportunity," he said as the elevator slowed. "And that everything you're about to do and see and hear is under strict confidentiality."

The doors dinged while I fought off the urge to be insulted. "That's kind of the job, Mr. Parker," I said, knowing enough sarcasm weighed my tone he got the message. "Since revealing client details is kind of against the law and everything." Who did he think I was?

He instantly softened, gesturing for me to exit ahead of him, Belladonna shifting inside the carrier as I entered the hallway, the soft carpet underfoot disguising the sound of my steps, elaborate white wallpaper with the black velvet design overlayed a little busy for my tastes running the full length of the double-wide corridor punctuated by ornamented white carved doorways with crisp black numbers identifying suites.

"My apologies again," he said. "My client has been betrayed before. I should have realized Dr. Renfrew would only recommend someone reputable and trustworthy. It's actually the only reason I agreed to allow the session." He led me to the right, stopping at a set of double doors at the end of the hall, the top floor's suites no doubt filled with the headliners of the movie. I'd only been in the honeymoon suite once, for a friend's wedding, so at least I was familiar with the layout. This whole situation by now, quite frankly, was less intriguing and more of a nuisance as I wrangled the cat carrier, my lingering irritation at being presumed a) entitled to a title I had never wanted, let alone earned, and b) unprofessional despite the assumption of my doctor status. I almost told Thomas I was done without carrying on any further. The pending session, I now was certain, would be nothing more than the entitled need of a pampered star to whine about things that other people would think were a dream come true to someone she deemed worthy of her complaining. Someone with a Dr. in front of their name.

Perfect excuse to skedaddle. Except, that lingering curiosity just wouldn't let me speak up, and while Thomas Parker did nothing to disavow me of that concern as he paused at the door, one hand on the knob, he at least had the honesty to allow his expression to shift to the faintest wince. "She's an artist," he said, soft and low. "They can be... temperamental. She just needs to be reassured. I'm sure you can handle that?"

He didn't wait for me to respond, instead pushing the door open and striding through. Leaving me to follow, now trepidatious and hoping I was up to the job. My clients all wanted my help, actually put the work in they chose to improve their lives. I only accepted them for that reason.

Which had me wondering what I'd been thinking as the tall, slim blonde, her near-emaciated body draped in a silk robe, stood to greet me, expression pinched and unhappy.

"Violet Hyde," Thomas said. "This is Dr. Persephone Pringle."

CHAPTER TWO

Things could have gone one of two ways. The visible unhappiness on her face, in her stance, in the entirety of her being, spoke of a deep-seated self-doubt more than likely created by the fame and false forms of attention the celebrated star and recent award-winner had spent her entire career enduring. One of the perils of being famous when not properly prepared for the pressures and ebb/flow of love and hate that seemed to be part of the hallmark of such a position as the people around her jockeyed continually for her notice and what she could do for them was the devouring fraud syndrome that came with even the faintest nuance of rejection, the continual need for more and more adoration almost like an addiction to heroin. The fact

Violet Hyde suffered from such an emotional and mental weight wasn't all that surprising to me. However, it was still to be determined if she was the kind of person who threw that weight around and used it on others like a weapon (more than likely) or retreated inside herself to a deepening, dark pit of self-judgment and horribly unappeasable lack of confidence.

Violet chose a kind of middle road, but only because of the struggling cat in the carrier I fought to keep level. With a squeal of delight, her face shifting instantly from that sullen petulance of hers into near innocent childishness, she hurried forward to crouch at my feet, fingers stroking against the mesh when Belladonna rubbed furiously in her attempt to convince someone to let her out.

The lovely woman looked up at me, smiling in genuine happiness now, pale blue eyes bright, her entire being glowing where once she'd borne her own dark cloud. "Can I hold her?"

"Of course," I smiled back, unzipping the carrier, Belladonna instantly hopping out and into Violet's arms. The actress stood in a smooth motion, turning in a circle to head for the sofa where she folded her long, slim limbs like a collapsing wooden model, snuggling the heavily purring white cat.

"Violet," Thomas said, "I told you about Dr. Pringle?" Why did he sound like he was talking to a child? Or feel he needed to remind her? Both items of evidence telling enough I filed away the information. "Dr. Renfrew—"

"Yes, yes, Thomas." She snapped at him, those blue eyes flickering with irritation, full mouth pulling down. "Just *go*."

He nodded instantly to Violet with a barely suppressed sigh before forcing a smile at me and backing out, closing the doors behind him.

The moment she returned her attention to Belladonna, Violet became that endearing girl again, though I knew she was pushing thirty. "She's *so* beautiful." Her perfect white veneers flashed at me. "What's her name?"

"Belladonna," I said, setting the carrier aside and taking a seat across from her, the cool, white leather of the overstuffed chair oddly comfortable as I sank into its embrace. I'd opted for just this side of a suit in a navy pencil skirt and pink silk shell, short-sleeved sweater adding just the hint of something more official and was glad I hadn't gone all-out professional. Violet's uber-casual flake-out on the sofa, all arms and legs almost smothered by white fluffy purring had me sitting back and crossing my legs, waiting for her to speak first.

"Belladonna," Violet kissed her forehead. "You know she's named after a deadly plant?" She laughed, a light but brittle sound while I smiled and nodded. I'd been informed by Thalia, as a matter of fact, the Vesterville heiress's passion all things growing, but especially the more deadly varieties. "I murdered someone once," Violet winked. "With belladonna, deadly nightshade. Only in the movies, of course."

"Of course," I said.

"It also means beautiful woman," she said, stroking the cat's ears and cheeks to the feline's delight. "You know Italian women used to ingest it to make their pupils larger, no matter it almost killed them as a result." Another laugh, though it was far from funny. "What we women endure for the attention of men." She sighed, expression settling into rather sad, but calm. "Thank you for coming on such short notice." Violet didn't meet my eyes this time. "I was hoping Dr. Renfrew would be able to join me, but he's apparently busy." She eye-rolled at that, laughed, the breaks in its authenticity more apparent. "I'm not the center of his universe, imagine that."

"I'm happy to be here," I said. "Richard is an old friend."

"So he said." She stretched out somewhat, as though relaxing in my company, a positive sign. "You realize this is spoiling me," she nodded to Belladonna purring and air kneading, flipped over on her back so Violet could rub her exposed belly. "Dr. Renfrew better have a cat waiting when I see him next time."

"I'll let him know," I said, "but don't get your hopes up. From what I remember, Richard is allergic."

"I didn't know that." She tilted her head, smile returning, small and secret and real. "Poor him. They are the best creatures."

"Do you have cats, Violet?" She shook her head as soon as I asked, rubbing her face against Belladonna's cheek.

"My life, it's hard." She stopped petting the cat for a moment, resting her long, slim hands on the fluffy belly, Belladonna chirping at her when she paused. Violet giggled, continuing her attentions. "Maybe I could make it work, though. Would be nice to at least have someone to love." Her voice hitched at the end of that sentence, right around "love" while she blinked quickly. Not hard to tell what her issues were, but I was here to listen and help if I could, not assess her. "Maybe if I didn't have to endure this wretched schedule." Grim anger gripped her, hands slowing but not stopping. "I'm so tired of it already, you know. The endless pressure to be here, do that, wear this, know your lines, do it again, more takes, do it better." She turned her head away from me, staring out the window at the summer morning. "Sometimes I wonder why they hire me." She shrugged delicately, met my gaze at last with a bit of guilt there, but wickedness, too. "I'm not the easiest person to work with, you know." She grinned then. "I'm sure they warned you, didn't they? Before you came here." They, as in Thomas and Richard? Or was she talking about the universal they of the judging public? "You're lucky you have Belladonna to soothe this savage beast." Violet kissed the cat and sighed. "I'm wretched, Dr. Pringle."

"Persephone, please," I said, not bothering to correct her. While Richard had gone on to a Ph.D. in psychology, I'd stopped at my master's before exploring alternative therapies and diving head-first into holistic wellness. Thankfully. I think carrying on into traditional talk therapy would have eventually crushed me. And while it wasn't accurate and rather unethical, I was a trained and skilled therapist, so if she wanted to carry on with the assumption or outright lie, I wasn't going to stop her.

Whatever she needed to feel comfortable. That was the job.

Violet nodded. "Do *not* call me Ms. Hyde," she said. "I *hate* that. Vi will do."

"Thank you, Vi," I said. "Now, tell me how I can help."

She didn't get to respond. The doors to her suite opened, a woman storming through, her frown aimed at the star who glared back, slouching even deeper into the sofa with Belladonna between her and the newcomer like a shield.

"You're due on set, Violet," the woman snapped. Glanced at me, at the cat, back to me. "What is this?" It was clear from the jeans, T-shirt and boots she favored this middle-aged and rather frumpy woman with her long, dark hair in a no-nonsense ponytail hanging out the back of her ballcap, not a stich of makeup or any effort to alter her appearance or hide the lines in her tanned skin, had nothing to do with goings-on in front of the camera and everything to do with behind it.

"I'm busy, Bronwyn," Violet said in the most condescending voice I'd ever heard anyone use. Like, so freaking cutting and dismissive and disdainful all wrapped in a near physical slap that I actually caught my breath. "Thomas will deal with you." She looked past the woman's shoulder. "Thomas! Deal with Bronwyn, won't you."

He hurried into the suite, clearly surprised to see the older woman there. "I messaged you," he said to her, gesturing for her to follow him out. Which she refused to do. "Violet needed some…" he glanced at me, "private time."

"*Private time.*" The woman's snapping rage might have been a hammer to Violet's delicate and precise dagger of attack, but it was no less impressive. "You have a contract, Violet." She ground that out between her clenched teeth, the two-way radio hanging from her belt squawking, cellphone in her back pocket buzzing continually. "I was assured these kinds of issues wouldn't be a problem." That was aimed at Thomas. "We don't have time or budget to waste on *private time.*" She only barely seemed to jerk herself under control but managed with visibly Herculean effort. "I need you on set. Now."

"I'll be along." Violet's languid response had the woman vibrating in rage, though she did allow Thomas to lead her out. When the doors closed behind them, the star tossed her head. "You see? You see what it's like? Even the director doesn't respect me or what I need. They only want, want, want." She clenched one fist but relaxed when Belladonna stood and head-butted her with firm insistence. Violet's quiet anger turned to tears, fat ones trickling from her eyes into the cat's fur when she hugged the feline to her. "No one loves me," she wailed.

There was the love reference again and, frankly, I was beginning to worry about the lovely woman who, for the next half hour or so, went on a ranting, emotion-driven and ominously unfettered wallow through so many emotions—from spitting hate for the costume department to weeping angst over the constant script changes into trembling terror she wouldn't get it right and wasn't good enough—I wondered at her mental health and just how anyone could let her perform in this state.

She sniffled, grabbing several tissues from a box next to her, and blew her nose while Belladonna leaned in and purred non-stop. "Persephone, would you be a dear and get me some water?" She gestured at the small fridge near the end of the sofa, and I nodded, complied, more than a bit bewildered by her overabundance of sharing, noting all of the bottles inside had been stripped of their labels, new ones in their place with VIOLET HYDE printed on them. I settled back into my chair and waited, the star drinking deeply before sagging as though spent.

"There's only one person on the whole set who cares about me," she said. "I'm so grateful to have Kole as my co-star. He's such a professional and we work so well together. I just adore him." She lit up, swinging out of her black pit of anger and despair in a way that had me wondering if she was medicated. And, if not, why not. "Have you seen Kole Ross? Any of his work?" I really had no idea, nodded anyway, just to keep her talking. That made her smile, hug Belladonna. "He's marvelous, so talented, such reach and expression. I'd have left on the first day if it wasn't for him." She laughed, low and rather sultry considering the circumstances, pushing her blonde hair back from her pale, hollow cheeks, gaze meeting mine with that wickedness returned. "He's been a great comfort."

I couldn't help but grin in return. "How nice of him."

She laughed at that, full-throated and back to her authentic self. Or, as far as I could tell, the woman she really deserved to be most of the time. Whatever happened to cripple her this emotionally—and yes, the lifestyle, her job, played a factor, but there had to be more to it—I wondered if Richard had managed to make any headway.

Violet was one of those clients who made me want to toss everything aside and do all I could to fix her. Not that it was possible, or my job, not really. But the need to try to guide her to healing herself was so strong it almost hurt.

Maybe because she reminded me a little of Thalia, the thin, blonde, pale, blue-eyed look of her, not to mention Thalia's fragility, and her recent increased retreat into Vesterville House, her odd behavior I'd begun to notice, the way she no longer seemed to shine as bright as she used to. The parallels between the two women only made my drive to act worse, not better. Since Thalia wouldn't accept help from me, maybe aiding this star could ease the guilt I felt over not being welcome to try for the sweet young woman I thought of as my second daughter.

"Thank you, Persephone." She sat forward suddenly, Belladonna perching on her lap, though Violet wrinkled her nose. "Nickname?"

"Seph," I said.

"Seph." She bobbed a nod at that, kissing the top of the cat's head. "And Bella, yes?" I nodded in agreement. "I feel so much better. You really helped. Dr. Renfrew was right, you're an amazing therapist and I'm so glad he recommended you."

Considering the fact that I hadn't exactly done anything yet except sit there and listen? Unsatisfying to the max. Trouble was, I didn't get to suggest we talk again, maybe without her director hovering, or her needing to be on set looming over us. Instead, as though he had been eavesdropping (and probably had been) the instant Violet proclaimed she was done, Thomas entered the room and, with a haste that had my head spinning, ushered me out.

But not before Violet hugged me after depositing Belladonna into the carrier. "Thank you," she whispered. Then spun and strode off, disappearing through a door and leaving me to walk out on Thomas's heels with a million questions and suggestions unspoken.

For now.

I had a feeling I'd be seeing Violet Hyde again.

CHAPTER THREE

Thomas didn't say a word until we were in the elevator, waiting until the doors closed on us, Belladonna meowing in time to the ding of the doors before he turned and grinned at me.

"You and your cat made a huge impression," he said. "I know she can be intense. You clearly did exactly what Dr. Renfrew said you could." He sounded impressed, continued smiling, his relief visible. "I'm sure our director, Bronwyn Carpenter, will be very grateful she can get back to work."

Bit of an understatement, if her anger at being delayed could even be turned around at this point. "Happy to help," I said. I was careful to keep my real reaction (phew, that was surreal) to myself because I was a pro, thank you, and it was none of his business. Even if he *was* her manager, he didn't need to know I thought the poor woman was a wreck who probably shouldn't be the main draw for a multi-million-dollar film let alone her own existence.

I was sure he knew anyway and since she was only a temporary client, did I really have the right to make such broad statements? Then again, wasn't he supposed to be looking out for her? As her manager, surely, he should be protecting her from herself. I sighed internally, realizing someone like Violet wasn't exactly easy to get along or negotiate with so the poor man had his work cut out for him no matter what. Maybe maintenance was the best he could manage.

If that was the case and this was his version of the status quo? Yeah, something was very wrong with this picture, and I didn't mean the film.

"I'm so sorry about her volatility." I understood his reflexive need to apologize, knowing it was more than likely he did a lot of that if her treatment of the director, Bronwyn, was a typical interaction. Again, this wasn't about him, but my client and I wasn't about to throw her (or my reputation) under a bus by gossiping or offering any indication the last hour was truly the most challenging session I'd ever encountered. Sure, I'd had the odd client who'd been sent to me via the prison system for evaluation, prior to my evolution into holistic practice. Dealing with sociopaths wasn't my favorite, but I was more than capable. But Violet Hyde's mercurial inner workings and the deep hurt she hid held a fascination for me equaling my compassion. Yes, she was horrible to the people around her, but I couldn't bring myself to judge her.

More than anyone I'd ever met; it was obvious to me she had her reasons.

Of course, I wasn't condoning her behavior, but I could see the pain triggering her. With the right treatment, Violet could find peace. Which had me wondering just what Richard had been doing all this time.

Him? I judged.

"I'm hoping you'll be available again if Violet requests a follow-up with you." Thomas's hesitation actually irritated me.

"Of course, I'd be happy to see Ms. Hyde again," I said, using her least preferred reference with him only because, again, professional.

He relaxed somewhat as the doors dinged and let us out into the lobby. Thomas paused at the threshold, shook my hand.

"Excellent," he said. "I'll be in touch, Dr. Pringle." Whoops, there it was again, but I didn't correct him as he backed onto the elevator and the doors closed on him, leaving me and my protesting cat to fend for ourselves.

Maybe getting a Ph.D. would be worth it just to keep assumptions at bay.

Like I cared one bit about other people's assumptions. Snort. My tattoos alone, climbing my arms and crossing my shoulders, were a roadmap to unconventionality, so anyone who chose to assume anything about me were welcome to it.

I turned to leave, pausing as Belladonna shifted her weight to the back of the carrier, setting it down to try to get her to move forward again. As I did, I stepped into the space next to the elevator doors and a decorative support pillar, partially hidden by a towering plant in an effort to keep the meandering guests from thinking I was torturing the cat. The second I set her down, two things happened. Belladonna went quiet (so it was motion that bothered her? Good to know) and two people approached the elevator doors, the handsome, dark-haired man mashing the button firmly with his thumb, angry expression only increasing his attractiveness. He towered over Bronwyn, his companion, the director just as angry but hers a bitter and ugly expression compared to his Hollywood grim determination.

"I'm telling you," he said in a lovely tenor, broad shoulders twitching under the light button-up he wore, hands clenched at his sides, "I'm at the end of my rope with her, Bron. You need to do something. These regular tantrums are making work impossible."

"I'm doing my best, Kole," the director said, identifying Mr. Gorgeous as none other than Violet Hyde's costar, "but you know what she's like."

"She's getting worse, not better," he snapped. "This is the third time since we started filming she's refused to show up on set. In a *week*." He crossed his arms over his chest, wide jaw jumping, dark eyes angry, full lips a thin line. "If I tried to pull that, the producers would have fired me by now."

"You don't have an Oscar for supporting actress," Bronwyn said, grumpy enough about Violet's success or distress or entitlement or all of the above loud and clear.

"Big deal," he snarled. "She can't win another award if she doesn't work." The doors dinged, sliding open as they continued talking, muffled as he entered but still audible until the doors closed on them. "I'm at the end, Bron. Either she goes or I do."

To my surprise, Bronwyn hadn't boarded the elevator with him, sighing instead in visible frustration, pulling out her phone. While I frowned down at Belladonna, a problem on my hands. It was pretty obvious to me that while Violet might have adored Kole, the feeling was not even remotely mutual and that, I knew, was a giant explosion waiting to happen.

I looked up at the sound of a new voice, taking note of the attractive young woman, as tall and thin as Violet but with long, dark hair and a fresh expression rather than the worn-out weariness I saw on the star upstairs. She'd joined Bronwyn and spoke with a bright and confident tone.

"You know I'm right here, Bron," she said. "I told the casting director this was a mistake. My part would be simple to recast. I already know the full script and I'm professional enough to show up on set when I'm supposed to."

"We've talked about this," the director snapped at her, not even looking up from her phone. "Everyone's heard of Violet Hyde. Her name is carrying this rom-com." She finally did glance up, fixing the young woman with a glare. "No one, on the other hand, has heard of Darby Buell."

While I stood there, my own anger rising at the incredible cruelty it took to say something like that to her face, Darby shrugged like she couldn't care less. "Not yet," she said. "You have Kole to carry the picture. What you need is a fresh face for the audience to fall in love with."

Bronwyn snorted. "Actors," she said. "You're all full of yourselves. Do your job, Darby, and stop trying to get Violet fired. You just don't have the juice, kid." The director turned and walked away, leaving the young woman to scowl at her before she hit the elevator button. I waited, uncomfortable and awkward until the doors closed on her before picking Belladonna's carrier up.

To her instant meowing.

"Let's get you home, sweet girl," I said. "We need to figure out a better way to do this." And I wasn't just talking about transporting her, either.

I might have been a stopgap according to Richard, but if there was a way to help Violet in the short time I had to treat her, you better believe I was going to do it.

Ph.D. Pffft. Who needed it?

CHAPTER FOUR

The moment I released Belladonna from her prison she scampered away from me, up the stairs and out of sight. I'd obviously been a horrible human and she couldn't wait to put as much distance between us as possible while she sulked.

Fine with me. I'd had more than enough yowling for the day, thank you, and it was barely 10AM. With the rest of my morning open (I'd rescheduled a number of clients with no idea how long Violet's session would take), rather than sit home and stew about my cat's unhappiness and the star's state of mind, I opted for coffee and company.

A quick text to the affirmative and I was out the door again, parking in front of The Blueberry Grill just as a dark blue Charger pulled up and took the slot next to me. I waved at my friend, Sheriff Cherise King exiting her unmarked cruiser like an action heroine, mirrored aviators hiding her black eyes, dress jacket and jeans today's outfit of choice. Not that I missed her uniform of khaki and black, but she looked far more like a cop in her casual dress as far as I was concerned.

"Nice boots," I grinned at her cowboy kicks.

Cherise flashed her perfect white teeth, dark skin glowing in the morning sunlight, pulling open the door for me, towering over me like always but seemingly even more so in those boots. "I'm trying to be incognito."

"Nice try," I snorted. "You might try crouching. Or not looking so much like a kick-butt superhero."

My sheriff friend grinned, sliding the arm of her sunglasses into the front of her t-shirt, black eyes sparkling. "You say the sweetest things."

We helped ourselves to a booth in the back, the Grill's dining area thinned out now that the morning rush was over but still full enough, we were lucky to nab the window seat. Moments later, a cheery and equally lovely young woman, her face the mirror of her mother's (even if Layla didn't get Cherise's height) bouncing to our seats in her work apron and golf shirt.

"What can I get you?" She beamed at both of us but held onto a modicum of professionalism while we placed our coffee orders, Cherise's daughter bopping away a moment later, her full head of corkscrew curls bouncing along to her beat.

"When did Layla start working for Ingrid?" I'd obviously fallen behind on news.

"A week ago," Cherise said, sitting back against the vinyl bench. "She loves it." The sheriff shrugged then. "Whatever makes her happy." She squinted at me, her smile turning wry. "Though, I do wish your kid wouldn't give her ideas."

Oh, boy. "Why?" What had Calliope done now?

Cherise glanced over her shoulder to make sure Layla wasn't on her way back before leaning in, elbows on the table, slightly worried expression on her face. "She wants to take a break from school." Ah, yeah. I could see how Calliope's choice to stop her business program might have influenced her younger friend, a year behind her. "She wants to travel, Seph. Like, not just the US. She's talking about Australia for a year." Cherise shook her head, pixie shining in the streaming sunlight, showing the tight bends of impending curls that would take over if she didn't wear her hair so short. "We're not saying no, but, well. *You* know."

"I do," I said, leaning back at Layla's approach. She set our coffees in front of us, took our breakfast order, then breezed away again. "You're worried." Not hard to carry on the conversation we'd been having despite the interruption. "She's twenty-one, lived all of her older years in a small town…" Yes, she'd been born and partially raised in Chicago, but they'd moved to Wallace when Layla was twelve, so her interaction with danger had been limited thanks to her age and Cherise's job as police detective. "At least she's talking to you." I hadn't meant that to come out the way it did, my friend grimacing sympathetically as she sipped her coffee.

"Yeah, I know," she said. "She didn't dump a scholarship and move in with her girlfriend and not tell me anything." Like Calliope. Thanks for the reminder. We'd come through most of that fiasco, but Thalia's seeming devolution into sadness and hermitage had me worried Calliope might not be the excellent influence I'd been hoping for. While opposites attracted and my extroverted and outgoing daughter always seemed a good balance to Thalia's reserved, introverted personality, had I overestimated—or miscalculated—the effect being together might be having on them?

"What does Martin think?" Cherise's husband, a family lawyer, had a softer touch than his law enforcement wife but was no less protective of their kids. Just like I knew my ex, SAIC Trent Garret, was of Calliope. Still, Martin didn't have the same background as my former husband or his own wife, and while my training as a therapist informed me of what the human mind was truly capable of (and not all of it good or moral or legal), he had a happier view of the world than the three of us.

"He's all for it," Cherise said. "Did his own backpacking trip when he was in college, thinks it would be good for her. So do I." She toyed with her spoon, rolling it over on the napkin covering the sparkly navy-blue tabletop. "We just have to trust we did a good job, I guess, and at some point, let them go."

Amen to that, sister. "What's with today's wardrobe change?" Not to switch out the topic, but I didn't feel comfortable talking about Layla when she could overhear. Besides, Cherise was right. Trusting that we'd done everything we could to prepare them for life came part and parcel with letting them live that life.

Cherise tilted her head toward the large window beside us. "Security's tight for the film," she said. "Logistics are kind of a mess, but we're doing our best. They didn't exactly give us a ton of warning." The first I'd heard of it had been two weeks ago. "I guess they were going to use another spot but kyboshed on short notice."

"It's good for Wallace," I said. "For business, anyway."

She nodded agreement. "As long as we make it through the next two weeks, we're golden." That's how much my head was in the sand. I hadn't even realized Cherise, or our town struggled to keep up with the production's needs. "I'm trying to stay under the radar so I can liaise with the production while my deputies and the private firm they brought in do their best not to annoy one another." Another grin flashed. "Guess how well that's going."

I could just imagine. "Look at you, using words like 'liaise'. Going Hollywood on me?"

Cherise snorted, tipped her cup at me. "Not as much as that kid of yours," she said. "Saw her on set this morning when I stopped in. She's in love, Seph. We might lose her to California if we're not careful."

Speak of my little devil, the ringing of the entry bells preceded the hasty entry of none other than the young woman in question. Calliope instantly rushed to the counter, saying something to Ingrid who nodded, then smiled and pointed in our direction, waving. My daughter spun, flashed a big smile, then returned her attention to the Grill's owner before leaving the two people she'd come in with to join us at our booth.

I slid sideways before she could hip bump me for space, Calliope exhaling a huge breath, eyes sparkling and a massive smile on her face reminding me my daughter was terrible at hiding her feelings. Heart on her sleeve? How about every emotion she ever felt?

"Production stalled, the talent's having issues. So, when craft services had a crash and burn with volume demand I volunteered to help." Her excitement had her talking a mile a minute. "I'm here to pick up extra for overflow." She eye-rolled like we should know what she was talking about and commiserate because she was industry now, babycakes. Not to mention we hadn't asked her why she was here or even got to say hello. "First AD and the DoP are clashing over schedule and if I have to listen to one more grip complain about the gaffers I'm going to *scream*." She laughed. "I love the movies!"

I'd be internet searching all of the above terms when I got home so I could keep up. At the moment, however, Calliope was done, energy resurging as she looked up when Ingrid called her name. I managed a hug and a kiss on her cheek, Cherise getting the same before my daughter rushed off, she and her two companions loading a van with the boxes of food Ingrid prepared for her before driving off, Calliope's merry wave making me smile.

"You're right," I said. "We might lose her." Sigh. "I'm worried about Thalia." I hadn't meant to blurt that out and if Calliope knew I had she'd be furious with me.

But this was Cherise, and hadn't we just been talking about our kids?

The sheriff hesitated before nodding. "I ran into her the other day," she said. "Layla was with me. She seemed… I don't know. Off?" I didn't comment, but I knew what she meant. "Layla says she's been quiet lately, that anytime she sees Calliope socially Thalia's not with her. And Calliope's not going out as much as she used to." Staying home out of loyalty? Now I really *was* worried. "She's been through a lot in the last nine months, Seph."

True enough, and, frankly, in her whole life. Losing her socialite parents when she was little after a childhood of neglect as the wealthy pair traveled the world was softened by the fact Calliope was her best friend and we'd pretty much adopted her as our own even before the deaths of Doncaster and Celia Vesterville. Followed by the loss of her family entirely in November, and her fears over the Vesterville curse, despite the fact it was merely a fear and not a reality, took a toll on Thalia. While her family hadn't been the kind one wished for, at least knowing she wasn't alone had to have had a stabilizing effect. Yes, we made sure to be there for her—Calliope especially—but there was a bloodline tie that couldn't be denied, good and kind and compassionate people on the other end or not. In this case, a solid not, with one exception and even that particular individual was no saint. "Did you want me to check in on her?"

I shook my head immediately. "Calliope would never forgive you *or* me. Because she'd know I was involved." Cherise sighed but nodded. "Just like Layla, I have to trust them and believe they'll be okay. At least they have each other."

Breakfast arrived, Cherise changing the

subject, asking about Mom and Ralph, her new husband, who had rented an RV for the summer and were touring the northwest. Part of me was jealous of her second chance at happiness, but mostly I was just happy for her. Which meant sharing the photos of her trip with Cherise and doing my best to stop thinking about Thalia Vesterville.

Not that it helped. As I climbed into my SUV, it took everything I had not to drive to Vesterville House, to visit with Thalia without Calliope present. Not that my second daughter would mind if I did. She'd welcome me with open arms, I was positive of that. Okay, mostly positive. Pretty sure. Oh, who knew with those two these days? But I *did* know if I made that trip Calliope would assume I was checking up on them. I'd already been chastised firmly for being a therapy mom despite my attempts to the contrary. The last thing I wanted was to poke my nose in where it wasn't wanted or welcome or needed.

Except, as I pulled into my driveway, I couldn't shake the feeling I was needed, even if the girls themselves couldn't see it and weren't willing or able to ask for help.

Distraction offered itself in the form of a hasty text I received as I unlocked my front door. *Jane Smith needs to see you*, Thomas Parker sent. *Are you available now?*

While I might not have been able to help my girls directly, here at least was a troubled woman I could try to guide to healing, futile or not. And while it meant clearing my schedule for the rest of the day and setting a truly terrible precedent that this could be a two-week panicked call kind of situation if I let it turn into that, I responded positively despite myself.

We're on set, Thomas sent. *Bring the cat.*

Sigh. Belladonna was going to murder me in my sleep.

CHAPTER FIVE

The drive onto the set was reasonably easy, guard at the gate taking a look at my driver's license before checking me off a list on his clipboard. It was hard not to rubberneck a little bit as I passed the small booth where he sat, driving under the slowly rising arm striped orange and white, onto the compound that had been fenced off at what had to have been an enormous expense. Fifteen-foot-tall chain-link stretched out to the right and left, a small parking lot filled with cars and golf carts, more of which of the small vehicles whipped around and through the collection of tents, structures and small outbuildings that filled the front end of the production's location.

I'd never been on a film set before, not

even bothered by Belladonna's meowing as I parked and exited with her in tow, passing between two large, white tents more familiar at a wedding than a film shoot, and into the hustle and bustle of what was, for all intents and purposes, a fake town.

Well, not the whole town, but sections of one, building fronts impressively realistic, the cost of constructing something like this truly boggling my mind. The adorable and classically quaint town center they'd created with its park-like round surrounded by cobblestones, gazebo in clear evidence, fountain and endless banks of flowers all central to what I was sure people the world over thought cute little American towns looked like. And none of them actually did.

"Dr. Pringle!" I'd stopped in my tracks and found myself gaping a little, grateful for Thomas's approach so the crew and cast who hurried around doing whatever it was they were doing didn't think I was some country bumpkin off the farm for the first time since birth. He stopped next to me, breathless. "Great, you brought the cat." The relief in his voice had my eyebrows rising. "This way, please. And hurry if you don't mind."

I had to almost trot to keep up with his long strides, Thomas not even attempting to slow down, passing the façade of a shop front to the plywood construct exposed on the backside. Almost tripped over a pile of black cords held down to the dirt with a metal plate, the contrast of the impeccably built small town fakery a stark opposition to the mundane truth that was dust, unfinished rear views of sets, wiring, lights, cameras and tons of action.

No time to get a good look, though I was certain my initial impression wouldn't be rewritten no matter how much time I had to linger. Disillusionment sadly accomplished, I focused on the task ahead, the line of RVs that reminded me I needed to call my mother at some point our destination.

Thomas stopped at the first one, a large and impressive beast of a trailer, the sides pulled out and a shaded veranda extended over the door. I didn't have to ask how Violet was doing or why I was needed, because long before I reached said RV, I could hear the shrieking.

Loud, diaphragm supported and truly tantrum level shrieking.

Someone threw something at the inside of the screen door, slamming it open and shut about an inch with the impact, the screaming carrying on, incoherent, though I did make out the word "script" in Violet's voice, so I made some guesses.

"Please," Thomas said, gaze flickering around us, cheeks red as I realized we were being observed, that cast and crew watched with various expressions but all on the same exasperated and irritated theme. "I need you to calm her down."

I wasn't sure she needed me at that moment, or even Belladonna, knowing it was more likely a couple of weeks off, some heavy-duty holistic therapies and permission to heal was the solution here. Since none of that was possible, however, and I'd agreed to this, my own drive to see if I could offer guidance pushing me onward, I nodded and headed for the door.

Pulled it open gingerly, peeking into the dim interior, letting my eyes adjust. Noted with some surprise Belladonna had stopped struggling and fell silent herself, as though sensing something that quieted her protesting. When nothing came flying at me, the high-pitched yelling over as well, I slowly climbed the stairs and stopped at the top in the small entry of the RV.

Violet's low cry was my welcome, the star throwing herself at me, though it was obvious when she crouched and unzipped the carrier, lifting Belladonna into her arms before turning and sinking to the couch she'd been stretched out on I wasn't who she'd been happy to see.

I tried not to feel insulted I'd been relegated to accessory to the main event, knowing Belladonna had a special instinct and influence over her that I couldn't compete with and didn't want to. And if all it took to steady Violet was a furry and purring hug, maybe the solution was much easier than therapy. Maybe she really did need to adopt a cat of her own.

Again I found myself setting aside the pet crate and taking a seat across from Violet. At least she acknowledged me now, proving it wasn't just about my feline companion, though honestly, I think she would have dumped on anyone who handed her a fluff and paused long enough to hear what she had to say. Which meant she poured everything out on me. Only, this time, instead of the mostly coherent thoughts she'd managed this morning, she seemed all over the place, lurching in impassioned rage to crushing despair to horrified terror to devouring doubt in a seemingly endless string of words that had me positive—without a doubt certain— she was either on the brink of a nervous breakdown or high on something.

This Violet didn't show any signs of the woman I'd spoken to this morning, no hints of her authentic happiness making appearances, no breath of the person she was without the pressure of her job and the endless and abiding pain she endured surfacing. Instead, the entire ranting process spewing from her came from whatever dark depths she'd sunken into and was struggling to surface from.

Don't ask me to tell you what she said. I barely remembered snippets, things about hating the script and wishing she was dead and wanting to kill people and hating her life, on and on until she was hoarse and hugging Belladonna so tightly the cat actually stopped purring and struggled.

And that was a terrible sign and had me moving to free her immediately. Violet seemed to recognize the cat's unhappiness first, however, and let her go. While she didn't move very far away, Belladonna expressed her displeasure by leaving Violet's lap, crouching next to her, looking up at her with her huge, green eyes. Violet sobbed, hands over her face, "I'm sorry, Bella, I'm sorry," making it through her choking tears and trembling fingers.

Whew. Maybe adopting a cat was a terrible idea after all. Honestly, whatever was going on, I'd had enough. Letting her rant was one thing, and could be helpful in certain circumstances, but it was clear to me this kind of therapy wasn't assisting Violet in coming to terms with what was troubling her and could even have been making things worse. So, despite the fact she wasn't technically my client (Richard could get mad at me later), I crossed to her and hugged her.

Violet hugging me? Totally fine, of course. Her choice. But me instigating it? Kind of against protocol, against a lot of rules, but you know what? The kid needed a hug and if no one else had the heart to give it to her? Professional conduct could take a hike.

Violet latched onto me in return, clinging to me, shaking and weeping, assuring me I'd made the right choice. Thomas peeked his head in, and I scowled at him, waved him off, though when a young woman I hadn't seen before slowly entered, her face sad, her arms hugging herself, I made a swift assessment of her posture and sorrow and gestured for her to join us.

She did, sitting where I had been. Violet had almost finished her outpour by then, though she hugged me tighter before letting me go. I stood, nodded to the girl who immediately took my place and embraced Violet, the star leaning into her, sniffling, while Belladonna returned to her lap and began to purr.

Reasonably certain things were under control now and another meltdown wasn't imminent, I ducked out, finding Thomas pacing by the door and, keeping my voice low, asked a few questions.

"It was the script changes," he said, whispering himself. "She hates change, especially on the day."

"Thomas." Bronwyn Carpenter, for her part, made no effort to speak quietly, the director stomping her way to the manager's side. "She's already blown half my day with her private time," she glared at me, looking me up and down, "this morning and now this temper tantrum? We have shots to get. And everyone else here is ready to work. Except your princess in there." She jerked a thumb in the direction of Violet. "I'm *this close*, Thomas." Her finger and thumb pinched together. "Get her together, or I start looking at new talent."

Not hard to note the young woman from the elevator earlier, the one Bronwyn called Darby Buell, stood nearby with her arms crossed over her chest and a smirk on her face. Despite the director's conversation, that expression could only mean one thing. She was poised and prepared to step in, make no mistake.

And honestly? I was pretty sure that was actually the smart option at this point. Didn't say it out loud, kept my mouth shut, while Thomas quickly reassured the director before she stalked off again.

She didn't get far, made it to the next trailer down the line, just as Kole Ross slammed out of his own RV, visibly furious. Darby instantly dropped her self-satisfaction and went to him, quietly speaking to him while he shook his head and stalked off, her on his trail, Kole calling for Bronwyn who didn't stop her forward motion.

Thomas spun on me. "I need her able to shoot," he said, his panic visible on his face, voice shaking. "Can you do it?"

I wanted to tell him no, that he was nuts for even considering it. The woman was a wreck. The fact he didn't seem to care, that the movie and his career and Bronwyn's demands came first said enough about the business I hoped Calliope got it out of her system before it made her this selfish and short-sighted.

"No promises," I said. "But I'll do what I can." For Violet, not him or the director or that young man who obviously misled my client into thinking he was anything but the fraud and backstabber he was.

My focus regained, I left Thomas to pace and returned to Violet with only one goal in mind: help her heal. By whatever means necessary.

CHAPTER SIX

The newcomer still held Violet when I returned, but the star seemed much calmer, stroking Belladonna's fur with gentle, shaking hands.

"Thank you for coming," Violet said, voice cracking and thick. She didn't look up at all, staring at the cat instead, shoulders slumped, the red dress she wore standing out, covered in sparkles, matching her high heels. Only now did I notice what she had on, full makeup a disaster, updo shaken partially loose. "I don't know what's wrong with me." She wiped at the mascara trail through her ruined foundation. "I'm not usually like this."

The young woman next to her winced. Okay, so that was a lie, even if Violet couldn't admit to it. I joined them, sitting across from them, reaching out to take Violet's hand. She clung to my touch, her free one sliding through Belladonna's fur over and over again.

"This is Emma," Violet said suddenly.

"Emma Fontaine," the other woman said, flawless makeup and blue streaked hair that matched her eyes adorable on her, the jeans and t-shirt she wore under what looked like some kind of utility belt not bearing tools of the construction trade, but makeup brushes and sponges. "I'm Vi's makeup artist."

"My only makeup artist," Violet said, managing a smile, still teary, lips trembling. "I never work with anyone else."

Emma nodded, smiled sadly back, hand rubbing the star's back in soft circles. "I'm sorry I wasn't here," she said. "When they gave you the new pages."

Violet shrugged, staring down at the floor and the scattered sheets extending the full length of the trailer. I'd stepped over them as best I could on my way in both times, but they bore enough damage already I knew anything I left behind wouldn't have contributed to the wrinkled, torn sheets of blue paper. "It doesn't matter," she said. "I'm not changing my dialogue now. The story doesn't make sense with these rewrites. I can't *work* like this." Her temper found its edge again, it seemed, face twisting with it. She grabbed the water bottle sitting on the counter next to her and took a drink before that surge of emotion could take her over again. "I *never* should have agreed to this stupid movie. It's beneath me."

"Vi," Emma said. "It was your contract. You didn't have a choice."

That was the wrong thing to say, apparently, because Violet shifted from weeping and angry but in control to a vengeful demon so fast Belladonna hit the floor with a startled grunt when the star leaped to her feet, throwing the water bottle down the RV to smash into the back wall so hard it cracked and sprayed liquid everywhere.

"I don't care about the contract!" I think that was what she said. "I don't care about this stupid film!" Again, pretty sure. "I hate all of it. I hate *you*!" She screamed that in Emma's face. "You're the worst makeup artist, talentless loser. Get out!"

Emma left, red-faced and weeping herself, while Violet threw herself onto the sofa, sobbing into a pillow she stuffed under her face. It took me a moment to gather myself, Belladonna surprising me by retreating by choice into her carrier and hiding there. So even my cat, the most patient and loving of therapy supports, had enough?

"Violet," I said after a moment. She ignored me, punching at the pillow under her, kicking her feet like a child. "Violet." She didn't speak, screaming now wordlessly into the fabric and stuffing. "That's enough."

She sat up abruptly, panting and enraged. Pointed one shaking finger at me.

"Worst therapist *ever*," she snarled. "Get out before I have you arrested."

There was nothing I could do. Any hope or idea or dream I had of helping this woman was gone. I had no choice but to go. Stood, zipping up Belladonna's case, the cat doing nothing to protest the move. When I straightened, I faced Violet down.

"You need help," I said, knowing the bluntness wasn't going to endear me but needing to at least get through to her. "Violet, you can't go on this way. Break your contract or finish the movie, it's up to you. But you have to find a way to heal before this kills you."

She didn't say a word, stared at me with hate—so much hate it made me shiver—I finally shrugged and left, heart breaking despite the casual gesture prior to my departure.

Because I knew I was right.

Thomas wasn't outside waiting this time and I was pretty sure that was a terrible sign. Kicking myself for mishandling this situation (while knowing I hadn't and trying not to blame Richard while blaming Richard), I headed for my car with my eerily silent cat. I spotted Calliope as I passed through the back lot but didn't bother her. She looked busy and I really needed to leave. Though, when I caught sight of Emma sitting behind a backdrop, head down and shoulders slumped, I paused to do what I could for her, at least.

Except, it turned out she didn't want my assistance, either, though she was much nicer about it.

"I'm fine, Dr. Pringle," she said, sniffling and doing her best to disguise the fact she'd been hiding back here, crying. I considered letting Belladonna out, but the cat's silence had me worried about her state of mind, too. "She's not always awful. She's just under a lot of pressure."

"If you need anything." I handed her one of my cards. "Don't suffer in silence, Emma. I'm here to help." Well, technically, I wasn't anymore, but I'd be happy to do a little pro bono for the lovely woman who put up with what she endured.

"Thank you." She tucked the card into her

tool belt, retrieving a packet of tissues and using one to dab at her tears.

"How long have you known Violet?" I really should have just left, but she didn't ask me to so I figured I'd do a little nose into unwelcome places poking while I could.

"Forever," Emma whispered. Then shook her head, eyes wide. "Just about a year."

Message received. "You really have to love your job," I said.

She shrugged, stood, smiled, if a wavering one. "I do," she said. "Thanks again." And walked away.

Which left me zero options, right?

That surreal feeling? Lingered while I sat in my office, Belladonna on her cushion on my desk as if nothing had happened. Even as I typed up my case notes to send to Richard. You have no idea how many times I backspaced on a turn of phrase or sentence of judgment, reading and rereading it over and over to make sure my frustration and concern didn't come across too harshly. After all, even he could only do what he did. The rest was up to Violet.

Tendencies toward mood swings, I found myself writing. *Recommend emotional release therapies, possibly hypnosis or chakra work and meditation.* It sounded flaky even to me, so I removed that part. He had his traditional methods, and I had my unconventional ones. Thing was, Richard and I never clashed over methodologies, however, the reason he was comfortable sending her to me. So, I hit undo and let it ride.

Whether he liked it or not, traditional talk therapy wasn't cutting it.

I was about to hit send when a text landed. No surprise, Thomas's panic came through loud and clear.

Please don't quit, he sent. *She didn't mean to fire you. Or threaten you.* I could picture Violet standing over his shoulder telling him what to write. *Can you come back?*

I thought about it long and hard, reached out and stroked Belladonna's fur. Sighed. *I'm sorry*, I sent. *Unless Ms. Smith is willing to engage in actual therapy, I'm unable to be of any assistance whatsoever.* I hesitated over the next text, a suggestion he get her a cat, and changed my mind. The way she'd squeezed Belladonna worried me, not that I thought she'd hurt a pet, but still. That tantrum with the water bottle?

I couldn't help the mental image flashing of her throwing my cat in a fit of rage.

Three texts later begging me was the limit. I ignored any further texts, added a note to the file for Richard I'd chosen to stop seeing her, and sent it to him. Sat back with guilt eating at me. Ate dinner with regret gnawing a hole in my gut. Went to bed with the temptation to change my mind and try again making me toss and turn.

My phone rang about midnight. Nope, wasn't asleep, not even close. A call that late always triggered anxiety, as if I didn't have enough already, the worry something happened to Calliope or Thalia or my mother always behind such a reaction. Except, I almost didn't answer the unlisted number because, my luck, it was a spammer.

Belladonna looked up, the ringing waking her. "Fine," I said. Answered. "Persephone Pringle."

"Seph." Her voice shook, tears aching in her words. "Seph, I'm scared."

"Violet?" I sat up, heart pounding. "Where are you? Are you safe? Is someone threatening you?"

"Only my own mind," she whispered. "Seph, I think I'm losing it." She coughed softly on the other end, cleared her throat. "I think I'm going crazy, and I don't know how to fix it."

That was it. The plea for help, a real one. I was already climbing out of bed and reaching for my jeans. "You're in your suite?"

"Yes," she said. "I'm so sorry, I know it's late. Can you come?"

"I'm on my way," I said. "Violet." I stopped in my tracks. "Are you thinking about hurting yourself?"

The pause was long enough my heart thudded painfully when she spoke again. "No," she said, firmly enough I believed her. "Other people? Absolutely."

Not the best news, but at least she wasn't suicidal. "I'll see you shortly," I said. "I'm only ten minutes away."

"Thank you, Seph," she said. "Don't bring Bella. I don't want to hurt her again."

I stared at my cat as I did up my belt buckle. "It's going to be all right, Vi," I said. "I want you to sit on the sofa, close your eyes, and take long, deep breaths. Just keep breathing until I get there. Promise me?"

"Promise," she said, sounding a little brighter. "Ten minutes, right?" So hopeful, so broken.

"I'm leaving now." I hung up, knowing I should have stayed on the line but wanting my wits about me as I drove and trying to treat her while behind the wheel just wasn't going to work.

It was the fastest I'd ever made the drive,

hoping no one caught me speeding, thankfully making it to the hotel parking lot without a ticket or delay. The elevator seemed to take forever to reach me, then even longer to ride to the suites. I tucked sideways and slipped through the moment the gap was wide enough, hurrying toward the double doors at the end of the hall.

Paused when I noticed one was ajar. Heart in my tight throat, I headed inside, tense, uncomfortable, a terrible, terrible feeling in my stomach.

"Vi?" She wasn't on the couch where I'd told her to be. Or in her bedroom, either, the bathroom, only a single light in the main living area giving any illumination. Enough, however, when I exited her room, I noted the absence of glare from the glass doors to the balcony.

Open, wide open.

I forced a slow inhale, stepped outside into the warm August evening, the sound of traffic, lights from the town illuminating the skyline. Walked to the iron railing, held it tightly in both hands. Looked down. Into the unlit pool deck and the quietly floating body in the dark water, outline just visible.

I don't remember how I got downstairs or pushed through the glass doors to the closed-off pool. I have no recollection of grabbing the skimmer and reaching out with it, pulling the floating thing toward me.

All I remember from that night? The serene look on her face as Violet Hyde gently bobbed to the side of the pool, staring up at me through dead and empty eyes.

CHAPTER SEVEN

I stood off to the side, out of the way of Owen Graves and the EMTs he brought with him as they lifted Violet's body out of the water. Cherise stayed quiet and close while I stared, unable to take my eyes off the sight, though I finally turned around, so I didn't have to watch. All of the other dead bodies I'd encountered had been only moderately painful to stumble over and disturbing to a point. While I know that sounds callous, I hadn't really known any of the deceased all that well nor had an emotional investment in their survival.

Violet was different though, obviously, and while she'd made more enemies than friends in her short life, I knew if she'd had the chance to heal, she could have turned that around. At least, that was what I told myself as I did my best to wrangle the emotional buildup that wailed about unfairness and asked me over and over again why I hadn't done more to help her.

"You said she called you," Cherise cleared her throat softly before prompting me with those words. Did she know how deeply this was hurting me? She must have, her own empathy like a superpower.

I nodded, thankful for the distraction, hearing Owen talking softly behind me with one of the EMTs, the quiet murmuring of the gathered crowd of watchers the deputies held off just inside the doors to the hotel making me angry all of a sudden. "Around 1AM," I said. "My call log will give you the exact time."

"Seph, is it possible maybe she did this to herself?" Cherise's kindness, while welcome, wasn't helping my state of mind or that very question I'd been trying not to beat myself with until I was black and blue inside.

If I'd only kept Violet on the phone. If I'd only agreed to see her earlier. If only I'd insisted on treatment when I'd first seen her. The problem remained, however, all of the what iffing in the world wasn't going to bring her back. Reverse the trauma or the tragic event. But guilt was the kind of companion that didn't easily step off in times like these and honestly, it was familiar enough it felt like the right place to settle no matter whether I held any responsibility for this outcome or not.

How sad to think remorse was a default when someone else's choices were the problem.

"She was in an emotional state," I said. "I did ask her if she was thinking about hurting herself. She said no, Cherise." The sheriff needed to hear me say it, though I wasn't sure why defending Violet felt so important to me. I couldn't disclose anything further, though it was true client privilege ended at death. She hadn't hurt anyone else, so divulging her desire to wouldn't help matters any. "I was ten minutes, max. By the time I got here, she was in the pool." I swallowed at the sound of a bag zipping. The body bag. "I searched the suite before noticing the balcony doors were open, so I went outside. I think I knew I'd find her here." I had to stop for a second, eyes stinging, hands beginning to shake and the thickness in my throat making it hard to breathe, to speak. "I shouldn't have hung up, Cherise."

One hand settled on my shoulder,

squeezed gently. "This isn't on you, Seph," she said, ever so softly, leaning in with her lips near my ear while I stood there and shook and fought to keep from sobbing. "You didn't do anything wrong. If anything, you tried to help her. How many times have you told me you can only do what you can do, and the rest is up to the person you're treating? She was responsible for her actions."

I nodded, swallowed hard, wiping at the tear that escaped, coughed around the lump keeping me from talking. "It could have been suicide," I whispered. "But please, don't make any assumptions, for Violet's sake." I met Cherise's eyes. "She deserves better from us than she got from everyone else in her life."

The sheriff squeezed again then let me go. "I promise I'll be thorough," she said. "If someone pushed her or lured her down here and drowned her, I'll find out, Seph. And, if she did kill herself..." Cherise sighed deeply, shaking her head, glancing over my shoulder toward the sound of Owen's voice. "I'm so sorry this had to happen."

"Me too." I hugged myself, forcing some deep breaths. "Thank you, Cherise."

"You going to be okay driving home?" Her concern and support helped more than she would ever know. "I can have a deputy take you, come get you myself in the morning for your car."

"I'll be okay," I said, pushing out a little smile. Turned at the sound of someone making a commotion, sorting out Bronwyn's voice as she pushed against the deputies.

"You can't just take them," the director was saying, angry enough I felt my own rise in response. Because she wasn't sad, was she? "They belong to the production."

"They're evidence for now," Owen told her from the side of the pool.

"What's so important?" Cherise strode to the coroner's side while I held my place, not wanting to get involved despite knowing I was already hip-deep and sinking.

"The shoes," Bronwyn snapped while the kick of her irritation fired up my temper. "She's wearing the prop shoes. I need them for production."

Was she freaking kidding me right now? But, before I could close the distance between us in a huff of anger, Cherise did it herself, striding to where Bronwyn stood, arms crossed over her chest, the tall sheriff towering over the director with her grim expression showing everyone present just what she thought of Bronwyn's demand.

"A young woman died tonight," she said.

"Those shoes?" She jerked her thumb over her shoulder. "The least of my concern. The fact they're the only thing you're worried about makes me happy your production will be leaving Wallace in two weeks. Or sooner, if Ms. Hyde's death puts an end to this circus you've brought to my town." Bronwyn had the good grace to look chastised, at least, if sullenly so, her dark hair hastily shoved into a ballcap, wrinkled clothes askew as if she'd fallen asleep in them. While I took in those details and my analytical brain assured me the director was under enormous pressure and I needed to cut her a little slack because surely, she did have a heart, but her reaction came from her own endless and weighty stress, I told it to shut up and keep its logic to itself.

The deputies made a path for Owen in his white hooded coveralls, the EMTs rolling the remains of Violet Hyde out past the crowd, secured in her body bag. I had to remember to thank Owen later for his forethought since enough cameras were out—the vultures, disgusting—that it was likely images of her dead body would have surfaced on the internet within seconds if he hadn't protected her from scrutiny.

Owen turned back after the EMTs made it through, joining me, waiting for Cherise who left Bronwyn to sulk and nodded to the young coroner as he pushed back the elastic hood and unzipped, slipping out of his blue booties and gloves and wadding up the disposable covering that I was accustomed to seeing him in. Weird I barely remembered what he looked like in jeans and a t-shirt, the familiar sight of the coverall at least lending him an air of authority while, as he stuffed the compressed protective gear under one arm, he looked more like a college kid heading to a frat party than a professional with a forensics degree.

As usual, however, he was all business and cut right to the facts, pushing his glasses up his narrow nose, dark curls askew thanks to the hood, dark eyes hidden behind the glare of his specs. "She drowned," he said. "Water in her mouth and esophagus. I'll confirm at the morgue, but if it looks like a duck, and quacks like a duck…" He shrugged.

Drowned, okay then. So, the only question remained, did she jump and end it all or did someone give her a helping hand that had nothing to do with saving Violet Hyde?

CHAPTER EIGHT

Cherise took Owen's rather careless analogy without judgment while I wanted to poke him for being blasé and callous about Violet's end. I glanced up as Calliope hurried through the crowd toward me, face pale, so pale, the deputies letting her through without thought. And that was typical small-town law enforcement for you, though I really wasn't complaining as my daughter threw her arms around me and hugged me tight.

It was only because I was looking at him that I noticed the flinch from Owen, the way his Adam's apple bobbed when he glanced at Calliope, how he quickly looked away, cleared his throat, and focused on Cherise with his olive skin pinking. Only then did I remember the weirdness from the flower show, how he'd asked about her. I'd done my duty and kept my questions to myself, but even Calliope seemed uncomfortable now, almost awkwardly ignoring Owen and using me and my grief as her shield.

Whatever was going on, they would sort it out, I knew, but now I had a million more questions I was kind of grateful for because they helped me shed some of my intense and painful guilt in favor of being nosy.

Silver linings wherever I could find them, thanks.

"No defensive wounds visible," Owen was saying, "and no visible ligature. I'll keep an eye on her, though, since bruising can surface over time." So, at least he wasn't jumping to conclusions about her death, right? That was comforting.

"Can you tell if she jumped?" Cherise looked up, Owen following her line of sight before he shook his head.

"If she did, that bruising will form over time," he said. "Depends on how she hit the water. If she dove in, there'll be no marks, but if she was pushed or fell and landed flat," he smacked his palms together, "there should be some damage that appears. The buoyancy of the water kept lividity from settling in, so if there is post-mortem bruise development, I'll see it within twenty-four hours."

"Thank you, Owen," Cherise said.

He bobbed a nod to her, to me. Hesitated just a little too long for comfort, hand reflexively adjusting his glasses again as he glanced at Calliope before he hurried off after the EMTs.

My daughter ignored his departure as if he hadn't even been here. But I didn't get to call her on it, more commotion erupting as Thomas Parker finally made an appearance.

"Where is she?" His frantic question had me frowning. I wanted to shout, "Where were you?" Held off, barely, as the deputies let him through at Cherise's wave. Violet's manager hurried toward us, rumpled and dressed in a t-shirt and jeans, no shoes. He'd clearly been sleeping and must have only now awakened. "I took a sleeping pill," he said, guilt in his voice enough to quiet my anger he hadn't been here. "It's been a long day. I can't believe it. Vi." He ran one hand through his messy hair, staring in horror at the pool. "Is she really gone?"

I let Cherise answer, but with a question of her own. "What time did you go to bed, Mr. Parker?"

He took a moment to respond, obviously distracted, finally meeting her eyes with a start. "Um, I don't remember. Maybe 10PM?"

I turned away, not wanting to take part in the questioning, knowing I'd be more accusatory than curious. Though Cherise had invited me to consult on cases in the past, there was a good chance I'd be asked to sit this one out and for good reason. I hugged my kid instead, letting her support me, while I turned away.

Noted the arrival of Kole Ross and Darby Buell, both of whom were barely dressed in robes, with that mussed appearance of people who'd been occupied with one another in intimate ways. The fact neither of them made an effort to hide their present state either meant they were openly a couple—not that I knew of—or didn't care if the world found out. Clearly, Violet's feelings for Kole meant nothing to him since he now outwardly flaunted his preference for the young woman who wanted to replace my client.

My stomach churned, anger returning. "I have to get out of here before I do something I'll regret."

Calliope wouldn't release me, holding me tight as if knowing what I had in mind and being the protective one this time. "Mom, I'm so sorry." Her round cheeks had flushed pink, lips drawn tight and jaw jumping as her expression finally settled into protective determination. "Come on, let's go."

Quite the flip in roles, though I didn't argue as my daughter took on what was usually my position, guiding me unresisting through the deputies and the crowd as phones turned toward me, a multitude of pictures no doubt being recorded. While it was meant to be hush-hush, I had no illusions my presence was any kind of secret, and I dreaded the social media onslaught, my mind spinning out scenarios and headlines of the therapist who failed Violet Hyde had me so tense I could barely breathe. Way to think about yourself, Seph, at a time like this.

The moment we passed the last of the onlookers, I did manage a breath, slumping against Calliope, feeling drained and sick. I made it through the corridor to the lobby but had to pause at the circle of seating in the center, knees shaking so badly I knew I wouldn't make it to my car without a break.

To my surprise, I found Emma Fontaine slumped in one of the leather love seats, weeping silently with her hands over her face. Having someone to comfort drove all other thoughts from me and, instead of the solitary seat I was going to use, I joined her on the couch, Calliope at my side, and gently hugged the young woman.

She gasped before clutching me close, shaking as much as I was. "She's dead," she wailed. "Violet's dead."

"I know," I managed to whisper. "I'm so sorry, Emma."

She pulled away enough to meet my eyes, hers devoid of makeup, pale green huge and bloodshot. "I can't believe this is happening." She sagged again in on herself, hands rising and falling in her lap with two soft thuds against the black cotton of her shorts. "Did she…?" Emma licked her lips, voice shaking. "Did she kill herself?"

"We don't know what happened," I said. "Not yet."

"I should have…" Emma stopped, coughed, sobbed. "It's my fault."

Inhale, Persephone Pringle. "If Violet did this to herself, Emma, it's no one's fault." Thanks for the reminder, Cherise. "And, if someone was responsible, the police will find out."

She flinched, shook, nodded. Looked like she wanted to say something, then stopped.

"Emma," I said, kindly but with firm intent. "Where were you tonight?"

Those green eyes met mine, hand falling to her lap, a pair of wireless earbuds in her palm.

"I went for a run," she said. "I can't run at night in LA, it's too dangerous. But a small town... it's my favorite. Any time we're in a quiet area, I run at night."

"Why don't you go lie down," I said. "I'll make sure the sheriff knows where you were in case she asks. Okay?"

Emma squeezed my hand, leaned forward, and did the same to Calliope. "Thank you," she said. "You're both so nice. I wish my mom was this nice, Cal."

"Did you want us to walk you to your room?" My daughter's compassion was one of her best traits.

But Emma stood then, shaking her head, exhaling a slow and trembling breath, sneakers squeaking on the marble floor. "I'll be okay." I stood next to her, hugged her again when she reached for me. "Thank you so much, Dr. Pringle."

"Seph," I said. "Get some rest, Emma. I'll talk to you tomorrow."

She hugged Calliope, too, then walked away toward the elevators, head down, arms wrapped around herself. I pulled my kid to me and hugged her, sighing out the last of the adrenaline that was all, apparently, that was keeping me going because I suddenly needed to lie down myself.

CHAPTER NINE

When I realized Calliope needed a ride, the company car she'd been using left on set when she returned to the hotel with the crew, I offered instantly to take her home rather than call for Thalia's driver to pick her up.

She buckled up on the passenger's side, my shaking subsided and the bone weariness retreating somewhat with our departure. Maybe I shouldn't have been driving, though I felt alert as soon as I sat behind the wheel. "I'm usually so tired after being on set all day I don't like to drive myself home," she said, mirroring my own thoughts when I powered up the engine and pulled out onto Main Street. "I should have told Cherise," she said. "I'm sure someone else will, but. Well, Violet had a lot of death threats. Like, all the time."

That was hardly surprising considering she was a celebrity. Death threats and trolling seemed to be part and parcel with the whole experience. "I'll let her know for you," I said. "But there's an excellent chance Violet…" I forced a deep breath, slowing it down and letting it out before going on. "That she committed suicide."

"I don't know, Mom," she said, frowning out the windshield, lips twisting. "I spent the last week watching her and she didn't seem the type. Aggressive, angry, antagonistic, bossy. She treated everyone around her horribly." She winced then, reached out and touched my hand. "Sorry, I know you liked her."

"I'm aware of her personality quirks," I said with enough sarcasm Calliope smiled.

"All I know is, she seemed more homicidal than suicidal," she said. Hadn't Violet herself said as much? Calliope glanced at me as I fastened my own seatbelt and sighed. "You sure you're okay?"

"I am," I said. "Just shaken." Part of me considered holding back, shielding her with a façade of *I'm fine* so she wouldn't worry. But she was a grown woman, and she deserved my honesty. "I gave up on her, Callie. Violet." She turned to me, quiet and listening. "I gave up because I told myself if she wasn't willing to help herself, I couldn't help her. Blamed my friend Richard for his lack of progress with her. Convinced myself she wasn't my problem. And all of that might be partially true, but the real truth is, I gave up."

"Mom," Callie said, stopped. "It's hard to be there for people sometimes, even in your job." She looked away, staring out the window, hands restless in her lap as her fingers wound around themselves as if seeking something they'd never find. "You taught me we might wish we could change others but the only person we can really change is ourselves."

"Nice to know something got through," I teased her. She flashed a grin, but it didn't last. "And yes, that's completely and utterly true. Does nothing at all to make me feel better right now, without taking some time to work it out, though." I glanced at her. "I changed my mind, went to help her and I was too late." Calliope nodded, her soft, brown curls bobbing around her jaw. "It hurts, even though it's not about me. It's about Violet."

My daughter's right hand rose and wiped her cheek very quickly.

In case you missed it, I wasn't just talking about Violet. Up to speed? Awesome.

Onward.

"Mom, I think something's wrong with Thalia." There it was, without me having to ask. And yes, I was aware I'd been a bit of a manipulator while being honest, but can you truly tell me if she didn't want to talk, if it wasn't on her mind, my kid wouldn't have said something unless she felt safe to do it?

"You're worried about her." I left it at that, hanging between us, waited for Calliope to fill in her own blanks. Whether she was finally ready to trust me after our previous argument over her privacy or was too tired to resist, my daughter nodded.

"She's been really withdrawn," Callie said, barely above a whisper, that hand rising to wipe again, falling to her lap when it was done. "She sleeps a lot, way more than normal. Sometimes she doesn't get up until after lunch and goes back to bed before dark." That sounded like depression to me, though I didn't say so. This was about Calliope getting a chance to give voice to her fear, not me offering useless suggestions or suppositions when they wouldn't help. First the vent, then the options. Though I'm sure she'd never know how hard the battle was in my head to keep my lips zipped on that drive to Vesterville House.

I'd certainly never be the one to tell her.

Calliope sighed deeply, scrubbing at her face with both hands before sniffling and helping herself to the box of tissues on the floor of the passenger's side as an afterthought. "It started right after the flower show ended. I can't even get her to go out to the garden anymore. Sandra's gone to work on the show, so the gardeners have been dealing with everything." Thalia's friend and head gardener, Sandra Lin was hosting a new TV show about deadly plants, something Thalia was supposed to be advising on. "It's like she's given up, Mom. She talks about the curse sometimes." The imagined Vesterville curse that gave terrible luck to everyone in the bloodline might have been a fallacy, but there was truth in the old adage that speaking things into reality and fearing things made them come true. "I'm pretty sure she's depressed, Mom. And I don't know what to do to help her."

I let that go for a long moment, debating before asking the obvious question. "Do you want me to talk to her?" A mistake, naturally. I knew the moment the words left my mouth.

She shook her head, looked away. "What I said before, about what you taught me. Change is the responsibility of the person whose life it is. Mom, this is up to Thalia, isn't it?"

So smart, my kid. Hurting and wanting to fix her love but knowing patience might be the only real remedy. I reached over and squeezed her hand.

"My darling girl," I said. "I love you so much." She blinked at me, lips quivering. "Thalia is lucky to have you and," I corrected her before she could speak, her intake of breath an obvious retort, "you are just as lucky to have her. And." I pulled up the driveway to Vesterville House in the dark, the gate opening automatically when Calliope clicked her opener at it, the front of the mansion lit enough it led us up the drive. "There comes a point when, sometimes, intervention is the only way to the light." I stopped in front of the towering stone house that reminded me more of a grim and judging castle than a home, putting the SUV in park while Calliope sat, making no move to leave, her hand still gripped in mine. "If that time comes and you think she needs support to find her way back, please tell me, Callie. I won't interfere. I'll just do my best to be here so she can feel safe enough to do what she needs to. To heal."

My daughter nodded, a tear dripping on

the back of my hand. "Thanks, Mom." She unbuckled her seatbelt, reaching across the console to hug me. "I love you too, you know. I don't tell you enough, or how much I appreciate the fact you've let us handle this on our own. If something happens, you'll be the first one I call, okay?" I nodded as she let me go. She managed a brave little smile, took another tissue. "She'll be all right. I'm doing everything I can to let her know I'm here, but she has to come through this herself."

I stroked curls out of her eyes, hand shaking again but for a different reason this time. "Tell her I love her," I said, voice cracking despite my best effort.

"I will." Calliope exited the car, closing the door behind her, pausing to wave before trotting up the stairs to the front doors of Vesterville House. While everything in my being begged me to go after her, to sit Thalia down and force the young woman I adored— both of them, frankly—to listen to me.

Instead, heart heavy, knowing it was the right thing to do if not the thing I most wanted in the whole world, I drove home with my anxiety level high enough at least I didn't fall asleep at the wheel.

Remember about those silver linings I mentioned before? I was racking up quite the collection.

So, you'll be wondering why, I imagine, by the time I parked in my driveway, my commitment to giving the girls space had died a harsh and painful death. Thing was, I couldn't help but compare Thalia's journey to the one Violet had taken. While they'd turned out completely differently when it came to emotional temperament, it was impossible to banish the fear that my second daughter might be on the verge of her own life choice that led to tragedy and despair.

Calliope could be furious with me for the rest of her life if that was the price I had to pay to ensure the mental well-being of the two young women I loved.

Being a responsible adult with a certain set of skills sucked sometimes.

CHAPTER TEN

I did manage to put some distance between that decision and actually taking action on it in part thanks to Richard. I had set my phone on silent while I was at the hotel, only thinking to check when I got home. Rather than just firing off a text, he'd left a voicemail.

"Seph, oh my God, I'm so sorry that this happened." He sounded faintly panicked, definitely saddened. Someone—most likely Thomas Parker—alerted him and shame on me for not thinking to. "Poor Violet. What a tragic end to a short but powerful career." Her legacy, while perhaps relevant to him, was beside the point as far as I was concerned. Who cared what she'd done? No one seemed to think about Violet as anything but a commodity. Knowing that wasn't really fair, I wriggled in discomfort as he spoke on. "I know the police probably think she killed herself, but Seph, she didn't have that in her, I swear. Vi was a fighter." I couldn't help but agree with him and I'd barely known her. "Her mother OD'd, and Violet always said she'd never, ever take her own life. That doing so was the coward's way out. I have to believe she held onto that because she gave me no reason not to." All of that reinforced my own assessment. "Someone did this to her, I'm sure of it. Look, please call me when you get the chance and keep me updated? I just can't believe she's gone."

I tried to reach him, but the line went to his message box, so I left a brief but detailed rundown of what happened and what I'd seen before hanging up and going to bed, where I snuggled my cat and passed out when the weariness of the day washed over me. Despite everything that happened, I slept long and peacefully enough the morning sunlight woke me to alertness I hadn't been expecting.

Friday meant only one client, and she'd already rescheduled, so I had the whole day to myself to get into trouble. An hour on my computer over coffee while my cat purred on her cushion was revealing enough, Violet's reputation preceding herself with sufficient evidence my experience with her wasn't new making me sit back and take stock of my guilt.

The last year or so, I noted, had been worse than ever, something Richard must have recognized himself. The assault charges she'd been facing against her last co-star might have been dropped, but settlements aside (you better believe she paid the young man off because the massive bruise and cut on his cheek would have held up in court), it was very clear to me everyone in Violet's life was aware of her spiral into darkness and not one person managed to convince her to turn that impending crash around.

Including yours truly, though I had to believe if I'd had the time to talk to her, maybe I could have had a positive influence. The arrogant ego in me chastised me while I pondered her life's story, from a poor girl raised by a single mom who died of a drug overdose to Oscar winner had come with so many knocks there was no way the rewards outweighed the continual punishments.

I squinted at the blonde cheerleader she'd been, trying not to assume she was the mean girl type and yet knowing in my heart that's exactly where she'd started out. When I clicked away from that photo, it led me to a post that sourced the image, posted just a few weeks ago on an anonymous insider blog that claimed to have all the dirt on all the stars.

The detailed and vitriolic deep dive into everything that was Violet had me scowling despite myself, no need to protect her any longer, after all, though I fought off the temptation to write a scathing reply to the disgusting and debasing accusations the author of the post outlined with gleeful cruelty.

No, I won't repeat what this individual wrote since I could barely stomach reading it, let alone letting it live in my head longer than necessary. Take it from me, the contents were beneath even the lowliest of jealous princesses who decided firing off horrible garbage about those who succeeded was their only path to fame. Because it wasn't just Violet who was featured on the nasty piece of work that was that particular slice of gross on the internet. I checked the dropdown on the list of posts available, seeing any number of famous actors and actresses listed, this specifically envious and evil creature happily eviscerating the most celebrated of celebrities.

Needless to say, the blogger's suggestion Violet's days as a bankable star were over was the only thing in their hate piece that rang true. I had a feeling, if she'd survived, this would have been her last movie, at least in the state she'd been in. I preferred to believe she would have taken time to heal and come back stronger and better than ever, but we'd never know, would we?

Too sad to contemplate.

A text landed while I clicked away from the blog, wanting a shower for my brain. I was surprised to find he reached out, immediately reading it out of curiosity as well as a morbid fascination with his thought process at a time like this. *Seph*, Thomas Parker sent. *I know it's a big ask, but some of the cast and crew would like grief counseling. Are you available?*

Huh. That came as a surprise, to be honest. From what I knew, aside from Emma, no one on set gave a crap about Violet. Still curious despite myself, I answered to the affirmative.

Thank you, he sent. *11AM, meet me at the trailers?*

That gave me a little over an hour, so I said yes. For selfish reasons, I'll admit it. As was often the case, maybe offering counseling to those who cared about Violet would help me, too.

It honestly felt like I was walking through

a horrible dream as I crossed the set and headed for the line of RVs at the back of the lot. Had I really only yesterday been here with Violet? It felt like years ago and yet as if it just happened within moments, that weirdly disorienting and uncomfortable press of time distorted by sadness and anxiety sitting on my shoulders despite the tools at my disposal.

The door to Violet's—correction, not hers anymore, was it?—trailer stood partially ajar so I entered, the sound of Thomas's voice luring me inside. He stood with his back to me, facing the rear of the trailer, talking to someone on his cell. He clearly didn't know I was there, and I was about to alert him to my presence when he spoke next, freezing me in place.

"I've already lost my meal ticket," he snarled, so far from the *please and thank you* man I'd grown accustomed to I caught my breath and stared. "I don't care how hard she had it, she did us all a favor jumping off that balcony. But now I need to fill the slot and I need it filled immediately."

I backed down the steps, stomach in knots, exiting to the gravel under my sandals, about to turn and just go. Because even her own manager was against her, no matter what he might have said, and I honestly just couldn't deal with these people anymore.

My feet moved without my permission or knowledge, carrying me to the end of the trailer and around the back where I bent in half, hands on my thighs, and caught my breath so I wouldn't throw up. No remorse, no pity, just a handout and what could she do for him and happy she was… yeah, if Calliope came to me and told me she wanted to go to Hollywood and do this full time?

We'd be having words before I chained her up in the basement.

CHAPTER ELEVEN

The RV rocked slightly, catching my attention and I quickly glanced around the corner to see if Thomas was leaving so I could make my getaway. After telling him what I thought of him and his lying jerkiness before insisting that he lose my number permanently. Instead, I caught sight of Darby Buell standing with Thomas, talking urgently and with intensity, joined shortly after by Kole Ross. Darby seemed to drag the star into the conversation, but he didn't resist, nodding and speaking up himself while Thomas listened with a frown that turned toward acceptance. The three of them, heads down and clearly conspiring, ended their talk with a handshake between the young actress and the manager before the trio headed off at a clip toward the other end of the line of RVs.

Whatever collective plan they'd made, it had to do with Violet, I was sure of it. Or the lack of Violet. Which meant I wasn't going to like it. More than ever, I wanted to be done with all of this, grief counseling for the cast a clear joke that I refused to be the punchline to any longer.

Except, I couldn't just leave it at that. As much as I wanted to wash my hands and book, I couldn't bring myself to do so with the cool confident decisiveness that was always my professional prerogative and really would have been the bigger person choice to make.

The trouble with wanting to do something and actually following through on it came down to emotional triggers and instinct, not always for the best. Which meant the whole feet controlling my brain thing? Happened again, strides long and angry as I pursued the conspirators all the way to—hardly a shocker—Bronwyn Carpenter.

"Fine," she was saying while Darby squealed and hugged Kole, then Thomas. "But only because I'm out of options. Don't disappoint me, Darby. We have one shot at this."

The young woman quickly bobbed a nod,

before spinning and heading toward me. She beamed a smile at me like I should be happy for her because it was clear to me what deal she'd made with the devil, while I wondered if she herself carried a demon inside her.

Before I could fire off—believe me, my mouth was suddenly as independent as my feet—Thomas took note of my presence and hurried to my side, while Kole drifted closer.

"Thank you for coming," Thomas said, gesturing at the man at his side. "Kole was hoping for a chance to talk. As was Darby and a few others."

I almost laughed. Choked on it, in fact. Held my temper by the barest thread as I turned to Kole. Noted the real sorrow on his face, and chose to be a professional instead of a psycho, because you better believe that had been the chosen path I'd been marching a few minutes ago.

"Of course," I said, though there was no warmth in it and I'm positive they both sensed it. Reined in my anger a bit more, jaw jumping. "I'm happy to help." Argh.

"Kole, you need to run through that stunt one more time before we shoot." Bronwyn didn't seem to care about anyone's feelings or need to talk. He nodded to her before offering me a sad smile.

"Thank you," he said. "I'll have a little time in about an hour if that's okay?" He pointed to the side of the set where a padded square stood, several tall, well-built men wrestling with one another in some kind of protective space where they practiced action sequences. "Just come get me then, if that works for you."

At least he was being polite. I could manage that, right? "See you in an hour." Kole left while I glared at Thomas. If he had any inkling of why I was so angry, he didn't mention it, instead offering that ingratiating smile I now knew hid a black heart and soulless evil as he gestured toward Violet's— growl, snarl, grrrr, *Darby's*—trailer.

Except we bypassed that RV and instead entered what felt like a remodeled construction site office, the metal container home to all kinds of lights and mirrors and hair and makeup artists who worked on the cast, Darby in the middle with Emma applying foundation to her skin. The sight of the artist now working on the new star settled the last of my anger. I tapped into my empathy as much as possible, coming to sit in the empty chair next to Darby while she scanned her phone as Emma did her best to do her job.

"Darby," Thomas said with a smile, "this is Dr. Pringle." I had no desire to correct him this time. Let her think what she wanted, like I cared. "She's here to help with the grieving process."

If I didn't know better, I might have been fooled, bought the show. Darby's smug expression as she typed something switched instantly to sorrow and worry as she looked up and leaned toward me, grasping for my hand, making Emma pull back quickly before she stabbed the actress with her makeup brush. As if she hadn't just smiled her way past me in triumphant delight.

"Oh, it's all so *terrible,* isn't it?" Surely an award-winning performance of her own, big, dark eyes blinking, long lashes already augmented with fakes. "Poor, poor Violet."

"Yes, a tragedy," I said.

"Though, you know, she was so troubled," Darby said, leaning back again, glancing at her phone. "At least now her poor, damaged soul is at peace."

Dear freaking God. Really? "I'm sure," I said. Because that was all I could manage.

"Everyone knows she was on the way out," Darby went on as those words echoed in my head and I made a leap. To a blog and a post and a horrible, nasty, disgusting human being who wrote terrible, hateful things about others. "It's so sad. She could have been a real talent if she'd just kept it together."

Okay, so never mind she won an Oscar and a bunch of other awards. And never mind she was the bankable star, not Darby.

"Violet told me she and Kole were a couple." I blurted that before I could stop myself. Gossip, Seph, really? Darby's nasty smile told me she was all for it.

"Oh, he tolerated her in the beginning," she said. "But he knew who the real star was." She winked at me. "Violet's been crashing for ages. It was only a matter of time before I took everything she had anyway." And now I knew why she wanted me to come and "grief counsel" her because she knew I worked with Violet. Classy and the perfect excuse for me to cut and leave. I was donezo. "Including Kole. And then she went and killed herself and handed me this role." Choke. "Poor, poor Violet."

Darby had no idea how close she was to a ballistic explosion of epic proportions. The fact was—and I wasn't proud of it—I wasn't really capable of keeping it together myself. The only reason I didn't lose my crap on the young woman then and there? The look on Emma's face. The internal battle she fought unsuccessfully with every word Darby spoke, her face crumbling and returning to red-cheeked determination before dissolving into grief all over again.

I reached out for the artist, but I was too late, Darby's final blow drawing out sobs from Emma. Before I could stand or try to comfort her, she threw down her brush and spun, running from the trailer.

While Darby frowned after her before calling out. "Can I get a new artist, please?" There was no kindness in the request.

As a handsome young man with the most amazing green eyeliner I'd ever seen hurried to take Emma's place, I stood and exited without a word to the star who, for her part, didn't seem to notice I was gone. In fact, I heard her laugh and chatter on her phone while I exited, ignoring the young man, the fake grief she'd attempted, everything but her own success.

She could have it, because in a few years' time, I had no doubt she'd be Violet.

CHAPTER TWELVE

The truly crappy thing about Darby's open admission about Kole? The fact was it could have been a trigger that led Violet to possible suicide. As things stood it was looking more and more like the woman I tried to help actually had taken her own life despite what she told me. I'd been fortunate up until now. I'd never lost a client before, nor a patient when I'd called them that. And while it was a selfish thing to think at any moment, it was also heartbreaking.

More guilt. Yay.

It hadn't been an hour, but I was in no mood to linger. If Kole wanted to talk to me about Violet, he'd better be prepared to do so now. Then again, maybe I should have given myself time to cool off since my head was now wrapping slowly but surely around the serious contemplation of his turn of attention from the former star of this particular movie and her replacement. Again, not that I blamed the young man or Darby for Violet's death. Unless one or the both of them had a hand in it, literally rather than emotionally. But I had a feeling neither was in any state of dress nor focus to have made the deceased star a priority last night.

I paused by the corner of the workout mat, Kole's carefully choreographed battle sequence (why they needed a fight scene in a romcom I had no idea, but I wasn't a screenwriter, so what did I know?) unfolding in front of me while all I could think about was Violet's call for help. When he looked up and noticed me, he immediately waved off his sparring partner and jogged toward me, a towel tossed in his direction caught with a deft hand, the white terrycloth turning faintly beige as the dust from the set and the remains of his foundation wiped clean. A fresh water bottle in hand, he stepped out to join me, expression grim and sad.

"Thank you for doing this, Dr. Pringle," he said. "I know Violet was a handful, and she didn't come across like it, but there was a time when she was amazing and in awe of this job.

She always said she didn't work, she played for a living." He shrugged his broad shoulders, catching his breath as he gestured toward a pair of folding chairs near the workout space. I took a seat, waiting for him to go on, which he did, another vigorous wipe with the towel clearing the sweat from his face and neck. "The work gets to you after a while, though, you know?" He kept his voice low, but it didn't sound like he was trying to hide anything, just wanted a bit of privacy between us. "It's harder for women than men, too. Our shelf life is longer. She was barely thirty and starting to get Mommy role offers." He snorted at that. "As if anyone would think Violet would make a good mother." He flinched when he realized what he'd said. Carried on. "Vi had a lot of issues from her own childhood." He took a sip of water. "Did you know her father killed himself when she was four?" I shook my head. "She found the body, sat with him until her mother came home from work. Hours later." He sighed as the hurt she bore finally had a source. "He'd shot himself. I guess she was a mess, quite literally, when her mother found her. I can't imagine something like that." He was going to make me cry without even trying and here I was supposed to be counseling *him*. "Don't get me wrong, I'm not making excuses for her." Kole sat back, water bottle balanced on one knee, the other starting to bob up and down, agitated jitter appearing. "She had a terrible temper, and she wasn't afraid to use it. I never understood her need to be purposefully cruel." He stared off into the distance, dark eyes lost. "I think I loved her once."

"She loved you," I said, wished I hadn't. His eyes fixed on mine, hurt there, hurt I caused and instantly regretted. "You meant a lot to her, Kole. I think in an ocean of people who only wanted things from her, she saw you as different. That brought her comfort." My attempt to cover my blurtiness could have gone badly. Instead, Kole nodded a slow and ponderous single head bob.

"Thank you," he said, quiet, pensive. "I wanted to be there for her. But this past year." He let out a low whistle, big hand running through his dark hair. "She went downhill, Doc. Like, crash and burn epic."

"Do you know what changed?" There had to have been a trigger for such a downturn, right?

Kole shrugged. "She won an Oscar," he said. "Maybe the hit of fame was too much?" He shook his head, taking another long drink.

"Whatever the reason, it was like she gave up on even trying to pretend she liked people, on patience, on everything. She could still act, but she was all over the place." His deep sigh held enough hurt I had to believe he meant it. "Thanks for listening, by the way. I really just wanted to talk to someone who actually liked her." His dark eyes held hope I was that person.

"I liked her very much," I said. "I wish I could have helped her."

He leaned forward and squeezed my hand. "We all did," he said with such earnestness I nodded. "Vi had her own path to walk. And it didn't involve getting better. It was almost like she gave up and just decided to be worse."

I was supposed to be supporting him, not the other way around. But I had to ask him, as cruel as the question was. "How did she take the fact you and Darby were together?"

Kole's wince was all the answer I needed, but he replied anyway. "She had a tantrum," he said. "I told her personally, last night."

So, he had seen her last night? "What time was that?"

"About 11PM, I think," he said. "She came to my room. Man, she was totally out of it." He slapped the towel against his leg. "She hated drugs, so I don't think she was high, but she was kind of acting like it. But wow, was she emotional. All over the place. When she saw Darby in my room..." Kole bit his lower lip. "She'd lost it on Darby, and I just couldn't take it anymore." Fear flickered, anxiety, worry. "Doc, do you think... did Vi kill herself because of what I told her?"

I didn't respond to that because I had asked myself the same question, right? "We still don't know if it was suicide," I said. "The sheriff is investigating the possibility someone pushed her."

His eyes flew wide at that, mouth open. Took him a long moment to speak and when he finally did it was garbled with emotion. "Who would want to kill Vi?"

"Good question," I said in agreement. "Any suggestions?"

Kole's gaze narrowed just a little. "I'm suddenly wondering if I'm on the list."

I shook my head immediately. "From what I understand you were occupied at time of death."

He blushed. It would have been adorable if the circumstances were different, gaze going down the line of RVs to the last one on the lot. "Darby and I both have alibis," he said. "I don't know what to tell you. Vi pushed a lot of buttons. Had her share of enemies, more than her share. She had this way of cutting you, you know?" My turn to nod. "Just slash you to ribbons with her tone and simple words that shouldn't have stung, but they did. They cut to the bone." He finished his water, tossing the bottle into the nearby trash. "I have to get back," he said. "We're filming this afternoon and there's a lot to cover if we want to wrap on time."

I stood as he did, shaking his hand when he offered it. "I'm sorry," I said. "I know I probably didn't help."

But Kole smiled, the sadness lingering, yes, but some joy there, too. "You actually did," he said. "And if someone did hurt her…" Kole's jaw tightened. "I'll do anything I can to help you find them. If I think of anything specific, I'll call."

"Thank you, Kole," I said. "Good luck filming today."

I watched him go, sad now instead of angry. He seemed like a nice guy, for all, a far cry from Violet and Darby. I didn't envy him this life of his no matter what the media tried to tell the rest of us about how awesome it was to be famous and rich and in the public eye.

From what I could tell? It was hell, not heaven.

It wasn't until I was on my way out, circling back past the workout space, I noticed the craft services food truck next to a white tent and a familiar face behind it. I didn't mean to head in that direction, but I found myself, clearly still in the grips of automatic motion dictated by my limbs and not my logic, standing at the counter covered in a variety of drinks and smiling at the woman in the apron on the other side.

Melanie Anderson smiled tentatively back, no surprise on her face so she'd clearly known I was on set. Of course, she did, since she was dating my ex-husband and my daughter was a PA. Surely, they'd talked, right? Besides, this was my second time here, so she likely saw me at least once.

"Persephone," she said, offering her hand, wiping it hastily on her apron first. "Nice to see you again."

"Hi Melanie," I said. "You, too. And not in a walk-by in Trent's office." That had been our one and only meeting not so long ago. I'd been angry with my ex, so it was likely that had come across to her, though I'd done my best to keep her from bearing the brunt of it because his stubbornness and refusal to give Calliope privacy and space wasn't his girlfriend's fault.

"Can I get you anything?" She offered me a water, a muffin. Were her hands trembling? Crap, I hoped I hadn't upset her that day. The last thing I wanted was for her to feel uncomfortable around me.

I waved off the offering, going for a full, authentic smile, tough to pull out at a time like this but I managed. "I'm on my way home," I said. "Callie didn't tell me you were working on set. How's it been?"

She shrugged a little, nodding to a pair of crew who breezed by and helped themselves before hurrying on. "It's intense," she laughed with a nervous trill to the sound. "I've never done anything like this before, so I'm learning, but it's been a bit of a curve."

Right, Calliope's trip to The Blueberry Grill yesterday happened because of an issue with food. "I'm sure you'll get the hang of it," I said.

She smiled back, nodded.

Can you say awkward silence?

I cut her a break and ended it while sighing internally. "Nice to see you," I said. "Say hello to my kid if you run into her."

Melanie's relieved smile told me she was much happier without me around, which made me kind of sad, to be honest. Especially if things with her and Trent were getting serious, and I had no reason to think they weren't. Not that his new girlfriend had to like me, but it would be nice to at least be able to maintain a conversation without feeling like I terrified the woman.

I was probably overreacting. It had been a heck of a couple of days, and I was done. Time to go home and forget about Violet Hyde and focus on the people I could help, right?

Sure, Pringle. Keep telling yourself that and you might even believe it.

CHAPTER THIRTEEN

Home would have been the logical choice, but since when had logic actually taken part in my decision-making in the last little while? I needed someone safe and friendly to unload on, an understanding, commiserating and unjudgmental shoulder to cry on, one I could talk about the case with and not worry I was spilling something I wasn't supposed to spill. See? I learned lessons given enough rope to hang myself with. Sorry, wrong analogy, but even learning lessons sometimes led me into trouble.

Okay, most times. You can stop laughing now.

That meant I had one option, not that I was complaining. Cherise seemed an excellent confidant since I could couch my griping in terms of the case, prove to her I was trustworthy when it came to keeping the beans in the bag, all while satisfying my need to vent until I choked. Sneaky, right? Thing was, as I entered the sheriff's office, it was right behind Owen Graves who flushed a little at the sight of me before saying hello in a soft, squeaky voice. Now I *really* needed to know what the heck happened between him and Calliope.

"Owen," I said, smiling.

He bobbed a quick nod back. Stuttered something I didn't catch. Caught his breath, cheeks pinking deeper, red splotches appearing on his neck and chest visible past the open top two buttons of his shirt. Wow, whatever it was, the embarrassment of it was doing a number on the young coroner. "How's... you?" He finally managed that question though it was more than likely he was planning to say something else and instead bungled the job. *How's* implied someone else, the pause a rethink and *you*, well.

Covering for something he didn't want to talk about? Check. A terrible liar who clearly couldn't hide his hurt feelings? Check. My daughter the source of his shame?

Oh, boy. Giant check, had to be.

I could have pressured him. Heck, I wanted to. The need to help wasn't gone with Violet, after all, just sore. Or maybe it made things worse, my failure with the star, that I was now seeing hurts that really weren't that big a deal as giant mountains of agony requiring therapy.

Deep breath, Persephone. Leave the poor kid alone.

Instead of badgering the poor guy, I let the fumble pass and gestured for him to carry on, knowing full well where he was headed. I know I was making him uncomfortable, following him all the way to the sheriff's door and all, but I wasn't going to hang out in the reception area and wait for him to finish. He could get a grip and get over whatever it was.

Of course, it occurred to me whatever had his knickers bunched and knotted was deeply personal and that he was running on the assumption my kid told me all about it. Why else would he be so embarrassed in my company? If only he knew Calliope had begun this new mind your own business and stay out of my privacy policy that meant I likely knew less than he did. No way to reassure him of that fact without coming out and confronting the mysterious elephant in the room though, so I guess we were just going to go with awkward.

Lovely.

I followed him all the way inside uninvited because I was in that kind of mood. Cherise didn't protest my presence, at least, Owen dropping a file folder on her desk as she stood to greet him.

"Perimortem bruising shows a pattern across her lower back," he said. "The mark matches the edge of the balcony. Which means she went over backward." He shrugged at that. "No real proof without being there, but it would be hard to fall from that position without help. More than likely, she was pushed." He carried on quickly before we could react to that. "And the tox panel says the victim was taking anti-anxiety medication, um, Zaxen? Though at two times the dose recommended, so she was out of it when she died." Wait, what? I'd seen her file, the one Richard sent me, and he hadn't prescribed her anything of the sort. In fact, he'd noted she couldn't take them for an undisclosed reason. Had some other doctor prescribed them in error?

Cherise thanked him while I scowled at the floor, losing my chance to question Owen as he exited quietly, gone with the closing of the door. I tsked at myself and let him escape, knowing I'd be cornering him eventually but right now too deep into the question of where Violet was getting medication she hadn't been prescribed.

"Says here there was DNA found on one of the shoes, on the surface. But the chlorine damaged it too badly to sequence." Cherise looked up with her eyebrows arched. "Which Owen failed to stop and tell me. Want to fill me in why he was in such a hurry to leave?"

I tossed my hands, sinking without grace into the seat across from her desk while she retook her own. "No one tells me anything anymore," I groused. Yes, it came out as petulance, I was well aware of that and no I wasn't apologizing for it.

Cherise flashed me a grin. "We had to go and have daughters with minds of their own." Her gaze returned to the file when I grunted in agreement—argh, daughters, *argh*—and went on as if her coroner hadn't scampered like a terrified rabbit. "Owen thinks someone pushed her, Seph." I looked up sharply, reminded of that suggestion he'd delivered so fast it was almost hard to miss. Was it wrong I felt a strong surge of relief followed by anger followed by more sorrow? None of which was doing me any favors.

"She was murdered," I said.

"Looks that way." Cherise sat back in her seat, the base creaking slightly as it tilted with her. "Anti-anxiety meds make sense, right?"

I shook my head, told her about Richard's case notes. "He didn't specify why. Usually, it's some kind of allergy. But whatever the reason—I'll find out and get back to you—she wasn't supposed to be taking anything like that."

"She could have been sneaking them." Cherise's full lips twisted as she frowned at the papers in front of her.

"Except if she was on anti-anxieties," I said, "she would have been mellow and calm, Cherise. Not an emotional train wreck." After all, that was the whole point, right? I pulled out my phone and dialed his number, but Richard failed to answer. Scowling over the fact he screened my call (or, more likely, was in session so get over yourself, Persephone), I instead called the other contact I had, putting it on speaker when he answered.

"I'm sorry I didn't get to say goodbye," Thomas Parker said. "I hope everything went all right?"

Wow, he really had the *shucks, I'm just a nice guy* dog and pony show down to a polished turd. I ignored his question and my urge to tell him off then and there and instead asked about the medication.

I might as well have stabbed him, he gasped so loudly. "Nope, no way," he said immediately. "Violet was not on any kind of anything."

"She could have just told you that," I said.

"No, you don't understand." He sounded like he was on the move, a little breathless. "Violet's mother started taking anti-anxieties after the death of her father. They almost killed her. She had a terrible adverse reaction and ended up overdosing on heroin after a massive battle with withdrawal from the medication." He stopped moving, but still panted a little. "Violet was absolutely against taking anything of that nature, adamant. She wouldn't have, I assure you."

"Then we have a problem," I said, Cherise nodding for me to continue. "She had those very drugs in her system when she died, Thomas."

"You're right," he said, "that *is* a problem. You're telling me someone purposely dosed her."

"And then," the sheriff said, interrupting the conversation, "took advantage of her fragile state and pushed her off the balcony to leave her to drown." Thomas's second gasp was at least as loud as his first. "Which means

I'm on my way to the set right now, Mr. Parker. Could you please have Bronwyn Carpenter standing by to talk to me when I arrive. This is now a murder investigation and I'm afraid I'm shutting down your production until I can discover who it was that killed Violet Hyde."

CHAPTER FOURTEEN

As I drove behind Cherise's Charger to the set, one thing was clear, especially after a rather panicked message from Richard. No way would Violet have taken any anti-anxiety medications of any kind.

His voicemail said it all. "Seph, Violet was terrified of turning into her mother. Nancy overdosed on heroin after trying to quit her meds. It's a rare reaction, but it can be genetic so she refused to even try any kind of medication despite the fact I recommended it. There is no reason on this earth that young woman would purposely take anything which only suggests foul play. Please, find out what happened to her."

He'd better believe I would.

That truth was only confirmed by her own

psychiatrist, I found myself thinking about sources the drug could have been administered through. Food, definitely, and drinks of any kind. Water? My mind landed on the small fridge in her hotel suite, the label-free bottles all marked with her name. If someone had drugged her on purpose, it wouldn't have been hard to do so. Anything meant for Violet might have borne the same specific titling, turning her every morsel of food and every sip into a possible delivery method.

I assisted Cherise in searching the trailer after gaining permission from a frowning Bronwyn who waved off the request as if delivered via irritating mosquito, the same RV that had been Violet's. Clearly, the director didn't care one way or another if we violated the privacy of her actors as long as we didn't bother her.

Maybe it helped Cherise relented and allowed the production to continue despite the murder investigation ongoing. I wasn't in the kind of mood to give Bronwyn the benefit of the doubt.

It was pretty obvious Darby had made it her own, not a trace of the old occupant remaining, and it had been only about twelve hours. We had about ten minutes to search before the star herself arrived, Darby's frown at our rifling through her things fair enough, I suppose, but still irked me.

"What did you do with Violet's stuff?" I didn't even bother to be nice because for all I knew I was staring at the killer. Sure, maybe she hadn't pushed Violet, but it was possible she drugged her. Had Kole do the pushing. After all, they were each other's alibis, and I was in a headspace of not trusting a single person on this set. Aside from Calliope. She got a pass for obvious reasons.

Darby shrugged inside her silk wrap, face still made up, hair in an updo but her wardrobe too casual for her styling. Clearly, she'd just come from shooting a scene, Thomas huffing up the stairs behind her.

"Trash," she said, nose wrinkling. "Where it belongs."

Seriously. Cherise interrupted, gloved hand shaking a yellow plastic pill bottle, the white label imprinted with Darby's name. "Zexan is an anti-anxiety med, isn't it?" Her gaze flickered to me. "How long have you been taking these, Ms. Buell?"

Darby didn't seem all that concerned about the find, which had me scowling. Though, she did step forward and grab the bottle from the sheriff, slamming it down on the counter. "Everyone takes something," she said. "Why do you care?"

Sure, she was an actress, and she could have faked that attitude, but.

Yeah. Pretty sure she wasn't the one drugging Violet. Didn't mean she wasn't part of the plan to kill her, though. I'd hang onto that dark thought for a while yet, thank you. Out of spite? Maybe. Probably.

That had me exiting the trailer and circling to the back of the lot where a row of dumpsters stood. Stopped in my tracks, frustrated and having not a single clue what to do from there. What, was I going to go through the entirety of the backlot's trash looking for something that might be Violet's?

Dumb, Persephone, and beneath you.

Someone touched my shoulder, turning me around in an angry spin before I realized it was Cherise.

"I'll have my deputies and Owen go through the garbage," she said. "We have somewhere else to look."

Of course, the sheriff had this covered and I was an idiot. I actually breathed a sigh of relief, feeling frustrated tears burn my eyes, knowing I was too deeply and emotionally invested in this for my own good but unable to stop myself from caring about the poor woman I now knew had been drugged and murdered. No one deserved that, no matter how hurt or cruel or seemingly broken.

I followed Cherise with my arms firmly clamped around me in a personal hug so I wouldn't fly apart, again trailing after her Charger in my SUV the short drive to the hotel. She handed me a fresh pair of gloves as we rode the elevator to the top floor, grim but kind.

"I should ask you to step off this case, Seph," she said, quietly and with regret. "But I know what you're like." Did she ever. I didn't even protest because I knew she knew I'd poke my nose in anyway. "Just promise me you'll share anything you find, and you won't put yourself in harm's way for once."

I snorted. "Never in the game plan," I said as the elevator doors slid open for us.

"That's the problem," Cherise said as we strode to the double doors still closed off with yellow police tape. She slit the seal and let us in, chuckling a little. "You don't mean to almost die. You just happen upon the opportunity."

She wasn't wrong. And her levity, despite the context, relaxed me somewhat so my thinking cleared. Made a beeline for the fridge and Violet's private water stash. Cherise followed, crouching when I pulled out a bottle and showed her what I'd noticed, that they were all marked with her name and seemed to have been opened at some point.

"I'll have Owen test these," Cherise said. "Looks like an excellent option, though."

A thorough search of the suite turned up nothing, not a trace of any medications that might remotely resemble anti-anxieties, though Cherise did the careful thing and bagged what looked like vitamins and a variety of supplements for sampling.

I lingered on the balcony while she finished, staring down into the pool, the water now drained thanks to Owen and the filters removed and taken to the lab in search of trace evidence. It was hard not to let memory transpose a darker scene with Violet floating below, though I finally shoved it back while doing the same physically, turning to rejoin Cherise.

She stood in the doorway, that compassion she was famous for almost palpable between us. She'd changed back into her long-sleeve khaki shirt and black dress pants, gun belt around her full hips, the white t-shirt crewneck under her uniform such a striking contrast with the gorgeous depth of her skin it seemed to almost glow. She always reminded me of a warrior queen born in the wrong era, and today was no exception.

"We'll find out who did this, Seph," she said. "You said that Violet was worse over the past year." I nodded. "And that her mother had a bad reaction to the anti-anxieties."

I almost smacked myself in the forehead, missing the forest for the trees. "She *did* have a predisposition, just like her mother," I said. "No wonder she was devolving. If she was somehow being dosed with Zexan against her knowledge, the side effects would show up in exactly the ways she's been acting." She'd been right to refuse to take the medications. "Whoever has been dosing her has been at it for a long time."

"Could they have been doing so in an attempt to calm her down?" Cherise frowned immediately, shook her head. "If it's been going on a year, they must have realized the effect the drugs were having and would have stopped if that was the goal."

"Exactly," I said. "So, it's someone who either knew her mother or about her past intimately and used the drugs to…" I thought about it a moment. "Slowly ruin her?"

Cherise was nodding, still frowning, hands on her hips. "If the goal was to kill her, why not just make her OD? I think you're right,

Seph. This isn't a short game. Whoever is behind drugging Violet wanted her to suffer."

I could barely comprehend such evil. "Her outbursts," I said. "They must have had her on a drugged and withdrawal cycle." That made total sense in the sickest way possible. "According to Richard, her mother reacted with anger and depression when she took them, but when she tried to come down, she was an emotional volcano." How cruel and disgusting did you have to be, how much of a sociopath, to purposely do something like that to someone? "Why they decided to kill her at last, though, that's the question."

Cherise pulled out her phone and texted someone, waited, only to have her phone ping almost immediately. "Owen said the Zexan test he did of Violet's hair confirms it," she said. "Aside from a few gaps, she's been taking it about a year according to the strand he sampled."

Gaps suggested lack of access, which indicated possibly someone on set with her, right? Meanwhile, a whole year of off-and-on chemical manipulation meant, I could only imagine, to ruin Violet completely, crushing her into dust before ending her life.

Whoever did this needed to go away forever and never see the light of day again.

CHAPTER FIFTEEN

The other source we hadn't yet sampled meant another trip back to the set and Melanie Anderson's craft services tent. While I doubted very much Trent's new girlfriend had anything to do with Violet's dosing— she'd had no access for the year required— her previous nervous state now had me wondering if she wasn't, in fact, afraid of me but had, perhaps, witnessed something that worried her.

Since she acted equally anxious around Cherise when we landed at her station, I was starting to wonder if the latter really was the case, only to have her react with shock and worry when the sheriff brought up the possibility Violet's food or drinks might have been tampered with.

"It's not like this is a bank vault," Melanie said with some haste, pale but for two bright points of pink on her cheeks. She gestured around her, even as one of the crew dodged in, grabbed a bottle, popped the top, took a drink, grimaced, put the cap back on and picked another, replacing the already opened one in the stack before carrying on. Melanie hastily removed it, but it was pretty clear she wasn't kidding. "I do my best to stay on top of things, but it's a bit of a madhouse at times."

"Do you supply everything for the whole set?" Cherise seemed about as impressed with the young man's lackadaisical treatment of the bottle he'd discarded as I was.

"Me and my whole team," Melanie said. "Mornings we use the big trailer," she pointed at the row beyond us, "to cook and prepare meals for the day. I'm mostly stationed here all day with others delivering to cast and crew as required." She clasped her shaking hands together. "I did have a few times when I needed Ingrid's staff to cover the shortfall, but most of the food and drink comes through me."

"What about the stars?" Maybe they had special treatment? "Did Violet Hyde have her own menu, for example?"

Melanie nodded, almost eye-rolled, made it halfway before her smile dropped as she realized, I could only imagine, she'd been ready to complain about a dead woman. Surely the flat and unhappy expressions on our faces told her to tread lightly, because her nervousness increased, licking her lips and stuttering a little before going on. Did I feel bad we were what amounted to bullying Trent's girlfriend? A bit. But Violet was dead, and I wasn't feeling very tolerant, frankly.

I'd apologize later.

"I prepared Violet's food myself," Melanie said. "She was very specific about ingredients and portion sizes." I could only imagine. "To be honest, she only ate once a day, so it wasn't much of a burden." Wow, really? "And she only ever drank water, no tea or coffee or anything." While there was nothing wrong with her choosing water over other beverages under normal conditions, I had no doubt she only did so to control her weight. Which was far too light for a normal human as far as I was concerned.

I was hating this career choice of hers even more.

"Did you ever see anyone tampering with her food?" Cherise seemed doubtful suddenly while I waited for Melanie's answer.

"Not at all," she said. "I would cook for her fresh when she asked and deliver it personally." She caught her breath, looking back and forth between us. "Did I do something wrong?"

"No," I said, finally relenting, reaching out to squeeze her hand which she seemed to welcome, though the extra tight grip she started with eased after a second as though she realized she'd overdone it too late. I released her before turning to Cherise. "It has to be the water."

She nodded. "Or the vitamins. Thank you, Ms. Anderson, you've been very helpful. Say hello to Trent for me if you'd be so kind."

Melanie flashed a relieved smile, dabbing at her forehead and upper lip with a napkin. "Of course, I will," she gushed suddenly. "He speaks so highly of you, sheriff. Of both of you."

That was nice of her to say. I almost made an effort, just to ease her tension further because it was clear now we were both the cause of it when the perfect person to interrupt bopped her way into our presence. Calliope hugged Cherise with enthusiasm, then me, grinning at Melanie.

"We broke for lunch," she told her father's girlfriend, a late call since it was almost 1PM, no doubt Bronwyn's doing since I knew she was tight on time. "Be prepared for the onslaught."

Melanie instantly turned and headed inside the little trailer, a threesome of people in aprons hurrying toward her and inside as well, before emerging in a steady stream like ants exiting a hill with plates and platters and trays filled with sandwiches, one of them struggling with what looked like a giant lasagna.

We hastily got out of the way as a rush of people headed in our direction, Calliope tugging us into a safe zone well back from the craft services mayhem.

"Savages," Calliope said. Then grinned like this was the most fun ever. "You two hungry?"

"Let's get off set," I said, Cherise nodding. "Do you have time to go to The Grill?"

Calliope's answering, "Yiiisssss," was all the answer I needed.

We headed out, deputies already digging in the garbage as we passed, Owen's familiar white-clad person heaving himself over the edge of a dumpster. Cherise left us to return to the office, which meant it was just me and Calliope. Normally I'd love that, but since I'd decided to go behind her back and talk to Thalia—never mind I hadn't acted on it yet because guilt knew no boundaries of time and space—I felt a little awkward with my own kid.

Hoping it didn't show, I settled into our favorite booth, nabbing it as a family of four left, helping Layla clear the remains of their meal.

"Brad's having a party tonight," she said to my daughter, Layla sounding tentative. "He was hoping you and Lia might make it."

Calliope's instant reaction, how her face fell before she forced her normal brightness back to the forefront told me more than she would ever know. "Probably not tonight," she said. "I'm still on set and the workload is mondo." She made a wry face that had Layla smiling in return.

"Sure," Cherise's daughter said. "I figured. I'll let him know." She handed us menus, took our drink orders and moved on while Calliope focused on her plastic-coated food offering selection like her life depended on it.

My cue not to ask a thing about Thalia. Proud of me? I chose, instead, to prod another sore spot that had me so curious I actually didn't care at this point of Calliope got mad at me for asking or not. "Okay, I really need to know," I said, leaning in and pushing the top of her menu down so I could meet her big, hazel eyes. She'd paled out a little, faint red blotches on her neck and cheeks evidence she was fighting emotions. Which meant teasing her could go one of two ways and I was hoping for giggles instead of fury. Took a shot. "What is up with you and Owen Graves?"

Calliope's mouth fell open and she inhaled sharply. This was the moment when I could find myself sitting alone after my daughter screamed at me for invading her privacy or catch myself from snorting as she collapsed into laughter.

I got about a midway reaction that leaned toward the sadly amused instead.

"Oh, Mom," she said, rather breathless, leaning in herself, clear indication she was open to sharing, thankfully. "It's so *awkward.*" Her exaggerated wince had me pretending bated breath at her every word. "He hit on me."

Well, whoops. "I hope you let him down easy," I said, trying not to smile.

She shrugged, sighed, sitting back again, now calm and relaxed and herself. "I guess he didn't know I was with Lia," she said. "Poor guy, he was a little drunk, at one of Brad's parties a month ago." She bit her lower lip, glanced around as if worried he or someone

Owen knew might pop up and overhear. "So was I." That didn't bode well for a happy ending. "He told me he was always attracted to me and asked me out in front of a bunch of people. Mom, how did he not know I was with Lia?" She tsked, eye-rolled again (her favorite, to my frustration when she was a teenager). "I didn't mean to be mean, but I guess I was. Kind of." Another wince. "I tried to talk to him, but he's been really weird ever since."

"The egos of young men," I said. "Far more fragile than they would ever admit. But Owen's a good guy, Callie. He'll get over it." I considered talking to him and discarded the idea immediately. This was definitely one of those situations where Calliope needed to handle the fallout of her actions. Just as Owen did.

Parenting, argh.

"I should have told you Melanie was doing craft," Calliope blurted then. "I'm sorry I didn't mention it. I never thought you'd have reason to talk to her."

"All good, baby," I said, sipping the water Layla set in front of me, giving her my food order before Calliope loaded up on her own. I didn't go on until Layla left. "I'm just grateful your father met someone and he's happy."

"He is, Mom," Calliope said. Hesitated, something in her eyes that had me wondering what she wasn't telling me this time almost prompting more questions before she went on. "She's the reason I got the PA job, you know." That sounded more defensive than grateful in case she missed it. "She recommended me when she got hired."

"That was very nice of her," I said. Left it to fall into the kind of silence I knew would make Calliope speak up just to fill it in.

"She has a daughter." Why did that come out almost like an accusation? I held off while Calliope tore a corner from her napkin and shredded it on the sparkly countertop. "Brin. She's nice."

"I bet," I murmured, leaving the door wide open.

A door that Calliope considered before inhaling and then firmly closing it. "I'm loving this job, Mom." The sparkle came back to her eyes, her voice, and I spent the next forty-five minutes listening to my kid rave about the movie-making process. And while I smiled and laughed and nodded and let her chatter because that was my daughter at her very best, I worried.

You better believe I worried.

And had plans to find out about this Brin

of Melanie's and just what it was about Trent's relationship with her that had my kid concerned.

CHAPTER SIXTEEN

I sat back at last from the delicious remains of my lunch wrap and salad, Calliope polishing off the final slurp of her chocolate milkshake. She might have been going on twenty-two, but she still had that cherubic look to her that made her seem much younger. Drinking milkshakes with her mom instead of beer? Only added to the illusion.

Maybe that was why it was so hard to let go and allow her to live her life without worrying about her. Sure, that was the reason. Snort.

"Mom, I'm sorry," she said, setting aside her empty glass. "I talked your ear off the whole time and didn't once ask you how things are going. With, *you* know." She tilted her head, lips tight. "Violet."

While under normal circumstances I would have probably glossed over it and just driven her back to set to carry on, I'd adopted this new open model with her and figured she was mature enough to handle it anyway. Besides, the more I shared with her, maybe the more she shared with me.

Sneaky, yes, I know. Carry on.

"Someone had to be drugging her," I said, keeping my voice down while Calliope gasped in surprise, one hand covering her open mouth. "I know, honey. It's awful. And there's evidence she was pushed from the balcony."

"Murder," Calliope said, voice low and anxious. Obviously, Bronwyn hadn't made that common knowledge on set yet despite Cherise's initial stop-work order. "That's horrible. Does Cherise have any idea who did it?"

"Not yet," I said, "but whoever's been feeding her the medication that's been altering her personality has been doing so off and on for about a year." Here, then, was a possible source of information I hadn't considered and though Calliope was only fresh to the industry, she was a smart cookie, my kid. "Someone close to her, likely who works with her on a regular basis."

She shook her head, visibly horrified. "It's like a big family, Mom," she said. "Yes, I know, Violet. And Darby's not much better." She sniffed as if the young star hadn't impressed her. "But everyone else? They all work together on the regular. It's kind of a traveling circus. Yes, there are new people all the time, but they tend to get hired on by the same producers and directors because they are familiar and trusted, you know?" I nodded, though this was kind of what I was afraid of. "How about Thomas?"

Don't get me wrong, he'd crossed my mind, but why would he ruin his own meal ticket as he called her? "Anyone else you can think of might have a grudge or said something that sparked your instincts?"

Calliope shook her head, brown curls turning faintly golden in the sunlight streaming through the picture window. "I'll keep my ears open, though," she said. "I doubt the fact Violet was murdered will stay a secret for long."

She had that right, part of the reason I didn't mind sharing. "Just be careful," I said. "And tell me anything that comes up so Cherise can deal with it, okay?"

She winked. "Oh, right, Cherise," she said with enough sarcasm it made me grin.

"Because she's the one who stumbles over murders all the time. Gotcha."

Smart Alek kidlet.

"I'll ask Emma," Calliope said as she stood, the two of us sliding free of the booth, my daughter checking the heavy black men's watch she wore. "If anyone will know, she will."

"Emma Fontaine?" Oh, yes. Right, we'd encountered her together at the hotel just before I drove Calliope home, thus the reason my daughter knew I'd understand who she meant.

"You know how close she was with Violet," Calliope said.

"Is she as authentic as she seems?" I didn't mean to sound judgmental of the rest of the cast and crew, but my daughter took it the way I intended. As we crossed to the front door, I waved to Layla, pointing at the cash I'd left on the table as she waved and beamed back. The doorbells chimed when Calliope pushed the glass entry open, letting in sunlight and traffic noise.

"She really is, Mom," she said, pausing to let a pair of pedestrians walk by before descending to the sidewalk and making her way to my SUV. "But we kind of clicked right away because she's trans."

I didn't get a chance to react to that reveal. My daughter spun with a horrified expression, grabbing me by the upper arms with both hands. "*Mom.*" She sounded sick, turned pale in the sunlight. "I did *not* say that out loud."

I hugged her quickly, felt her trembling. "It's me, Callie," I whispered. "You can tell me anything."

"It's not mine to *tell*," she whispered back, choked up. Pulled away, shaking her head so hard her curls bounced. "I can't believe I *did* that." She shoved both hands into the back pockets of her jeans, misery clear on her face. "I'm still getting used to, you know. Being who I am." I nodded, let her work her way through it. "But that's no excuse for outing someone."

"I get that," I said, stroking her arm. "I swear she'll never know you told me. Honey, it's been a big year for you and for Thalia. You're allowed to make mistakes, you know. It's going to happen. I know you would never hurt another person on purpose." She blinked at me, mute and definitely judging herself but listening at least. "Tell Emma you told me and apologize. I know she'll be okay with it. And if she's not, that's all right, too. But if you were going to tell anyone, you know I'm the perfect one to make that particular mistake with, so you'll remember to never do it again."

She nodded finally, hugged me again, this time so hard around the neck I choked a little. But she relented at last, climbed into the SUV without saying another word. Was pretty much silent the rest of the drive back, too. Until I parked in the lot and waited for her to exit.

She turned to me at last, composure returned. "Thanks, Mom," she said. Simple, plain, clean. But with a million emotions behind her eyes.

Bratty child. She had to go and make me cry.

Calliope left without another word and I drove home. I'm not ashamed to admit it took the majority of the drive to let out the leaking, happy tears her gratitude triggered. I took a moment to dab at my mascara and blow my nose before going into the house, Belladonna keening at me for food, naturally, which she got in abundance, her own whole can of tuna, while I sat at the counter and thought about my amazing kid.

Which led me to think about Emma. Honestly, I would have never known she'd physically transitioned to her true gender. It was clear to me she'd made that transition successfully, which made me very happy for her. There was more than enough hate and homophobia in the world I worried about my kid and her girlfriend, but the horrific attacks and increasing transphobia in the world had my heart going out even more to Emma. Choosing to turn her back on the physical gender she was born with for her truth had to have been one of the hardest and most gratifying decisions of her life. Seeing that she not just passed (I personally didn't like that term because it meant she was faking, which I knew she wasn't) but fully embodied who she was born to be felt like at least a little vindication.

I'd had enough trans men and women clients over the years I knew that wasn't always the case, though why so many took such offense to another person's choice to be who they were meant to be always baffled me. While we had great capacity for love and caring, human beings were also the epitome of cruelty.

Knowing how hard she'd likely had it, I couldn't help the next string of thoughts that woke my guilt all over again and had me chastising myself for jumping to conclusions while doing an internet search on Emma Fontaine. Easy enough to find and review her professional page and, to my surprise, her blog and her openness about her journey from her previous life to the present. While she didn't use her dead name (good for her), she didn't flinch from sharing images of herself in her prior incarnation, before the hormones and the surgeries that connected her body to her spirit. That was why, as I perused the images, those thoughts I'd been having that brought on the waves of guilt overwhelmed any chance said guilt had of making me stop digging and, instead, brought about an *ah-ha* moment.

A very sad *ah-ha* at that.

Because the high school logo and mascot from Violet's cheerleader days I'd seen only yesterday was the exact same logo and mascot in Emma's senior photo. And they didn't just attend the same school, oh no.

They were in the same graduating class.

Even more damning? One of Emma's first blog posts, titled *GUILTY*, in which she accused several of the popular kids—Violet among them—of bullying her best friend, a young gay man, into killing himself. No charges were brought, I realized when I looked up the local newspaper articles. In fact, after a single mention, the whole death was ignored by town media.

Oh, Emma.

I studied the pictures she'd posted of what she used to look like and sighed. There was no way Violet could have known it was the same person. Unless Emma told her? But why would she? They were far from friends, after all, and I couldn't imagine Emma herself escaped high school unscathed by the derisive and hateful rhetoric the more popular kids slung to make themselves feel superior.

Why would Emma volunteer, then, to be Violet's personal makeup artist unless it was for a chance at revenge? And didn't she say she'd known Violet forever—a fact I'd passed off as a reference to it feeling that way, not being that way—and then corrected to say she'd worked with the star for a year.

I hated how things were looking, but honestly, Emma's trans status aside, I couldn't let guilt stop me from finding the truth about who drugged and killed Violet. Even if that person had been through enough in her life already for a thousand people and really believed the fallen movie star deserved it.

CHAPTER SEVENTEEN

My text to Cherise on the topic returned some equally interesting information.

Both Kole Ross and Thomas Parker have a prescription for Zexan, the sheriff sent. *As do a handful of the minor cast and crew. Seph, including Melanie Anderson.*

Huh. Well, I'd already reassured myself Trent's girlfriend had nothing to do with Violet's death, though from her obvious nervousness there was a good reason for her to take anti-anxieties, I guess.

Emma Fontaine? I held my breath before Cherise's answer came back.

Nope, not that I was able to find, she sent. Phew, so I had jumped to a conclusion. Sorry, Emma. *Turns out Bronwyn Carpenter has a bit of a rep herself,* Cherise sent. *Trouble with prescription drugs and alcohol, though she was an oxy addict, no Zexan.* Yikes, this business really did a number on people. *But she's been clean for a year, supposedly.* A coincidence? *This is her first film with Violet.* Ah, so she'd thought of that, too. *Sounds like it's her fast track back to the big times.* Which meant she was off the suspect list. Why kill the golden goose? *I'll look into Emma*, Cherise sent before wrapping up with a question of her own. *I may have missed something. Anything else come up?*

Not yet, I sent, feeling a little guilty myself for outing the young woman as trans to my sheriff friend, though how could I not, under the circumstances? I comforted myself with the fact Emma was so open about her transition, but it still didn't sit right. *Keep me posted?*

Will do. Cherise signed off while I sat in the sunlit kitchen, restless, knees jittering like I'd had too much coffee when the opposite was true, while a familiar and beloved face surfaced, one I was sure I could save.

Knowing how much trouble I'd be in when (oh, you better believe *when*) Calliope found out, I packed up Belladonna and headed for Vesterville House.

I knew already, okay? You didn't have to say it. Thing was, I'd already made up my mind I was going to talk to Thalia, so it's not like you should be surprised to discover I pulled into the driveway ten minutes later after a short chat at the gate with Lloyd, the butler and retired CIA agent who guarded all things Vesterville.

She didn't meet me at the door. That was worrying in itself, Lloyd's lined face drawn and worried as I carried the silent Belladonna into the house via her carrier. The fact she hadn't meeped or shown a glimmer of unhappiness on the drive over had me hopeful she'd at least resigned herself to the fact the container was now a way of life for her if she wanted to travel with me. But her comfort wasn't on my mind at the moment.

"How is she?" I paused to squeeze Lloyd's upper arm, to ask in a lowered voice the question Calliope didn't fully answer.

"Troubled, Ms. Pringle," he said, voice sad. "I know she'll be happy to see you, however."

I wasn't so sure, though as I followed him through the towering, dark wooded foyer, the black marble underfoot sliding under my sandals, I hoped I was wrong. Maybe she hadn't come to the door for a reason as yet undiscovered and here I was just jumping to conclusions.

As it turned out, she sat on the window seat of the sitting room, looking out at the garden, her slim, almost emaciated, body wrapped in a fluffy blanket. Despite the August warmth outside, the house had a distinct chill that only old, cold stone walls could impart. I waved off Lloyd before he could announce me, smiling as he closed the door and left me to whatever it was I'd come here to do. Because right now, I wasn't sure what that might end up being.

Without making a gigantic mess.

Before I could decide how to approach her (bright and smiling, quiet and compassionate, sad and worried) Belladonna made the choice for me. With an extended meow of pure misery, she began scratching the mesh front hard enough I worried she might rip the strong loops of fabric.

Thalia turned instantly, the backlight of the sun casting her pale blonde hair in a haloed pool of light around her shadowed face. With a low cry, she discarded the blanket and hurried toward us, hugging me quickly before bending to unzip the carrier and lift Belladonna out.

Instant purrathon all while those green eyes glared at me like this was my fault.

Hard not to draw parallels to the pale and

lovely young woman in front of me, another tall, thin blonde holding a purring cat while staring at me with giant blue eyes full of hurt. It choked me up, I couldn't help it, and with another soft moan of her own pain expressed, Thalia embraced me with my cat between us, vibration shivering through to my bones.

"Seph," Thalia whispered. "I'm sorry I haven't seen you lately." She pulled away, gestured gracefully for me to join her on the sofa, sitting crossed-legged with a pillow in her lap for Belladonna to perch on while I scooted in next to her, knees touching.

"I'm worried about you," I said, rather than pussyfoot because I wasn't good at pussyfooting, and she knew better anyway. Why I was here. She had to, from the sorrow on her face, lingering even when she smiled at Belladonna who headbutted her hand for more scratches. There was a fresh hollowness to Thalia's cheeks, her skin almost translucent, faint blue veins showing beneath. And while she'd always been pale, she looked like she was fading away.

Calliope wasn't going to get a chance to be angry with me for poking my nose in. I had dibs on that department.

"I'm… feeling out of sorts," Thalia said. "I know what you're thinking." She flashed a

Thalia smile, the hint of her there if her heart was still on the missing list. "I'm well aware of the fact I'm probably depressed. It's okay. I need to work through it, don't I?"

Ooooh, she had to turn therapy talk on me. "You do," I said. "But there's nothing to say you can't have help, Thalia. And tools."

She snuggled the cat suddenly. "And Belladonna?" There she was, wicked gleam behind her eyes, laugh making her surface, if only for a delightful moment. And then she was gone again, sagging over the fluffy white feline. "Callie's having so much fun on set," she said. "Talks about how wonderful it is. She's so full of energy all the time and I'm tired, Seph." Her hands dove deep into Belladonna's fur. "Like I can't muster any interest or enthusiasm for anything. I'm not feeling sad, really, just sort of... empty."

My therapist's mind logically murmured *classic depression* while my mom brain screamed *HELP HER!* "Have you talked to anyone?" She opened her mouth, but I knew what she was going to say. "Anyone but Callie?" This time her lips closed, and she shook her head. "You don't have to choose me, you know," I said. "I won't be hurt, Thalia. But you need to talk to someone."

"I just had a checkup a month ago," she

offered tentatively. "He said I was just fine physically."

Uh-huh. "Listen." I drew a breath, pulled myself together and fixed her with a firm stare. "This kind of thing doesn't have to be a giant deal. Everyone goes through times of mental health issues, whether they want to admit it or not. The only times it gets out of hand are when there are underlying untreated chemical or physiological issues. Or when the person refuses to accept or address how they are feeling."

Thalia looked away almost immediately, staring at the purring cat whose giant green eyes stared back into hers. "I know." The most frustrating two words ever uttered.

"It's the curse, Seph." I kind of expected that but not the way she delivered it. Frightened, like a child afraid of the Boogeyman coming for her in the dark. "It sits on me. Weighs me down. I know you don't think it's real, but it is." She finally looked up again, tears on her cheeks. "And it's going to get me, too."

Had she said this to Calliope and my daughter still didn't come to me for help? I was going to kick her behind.

"How about a change of scenery?" She didn't have to live here, after all. She had enough money at her disposal to own palatial mansions in any number of cities or countries around the world and have lots left over. "Thalia, you don't have to stay here."

She perked at that like she hadn't considered it a possibility. Then slouched again. "Callie's working," she said. "She needs to be here."

"For a couple of weeks," I said. "You two could plan a trip, maybe." The paleness in her cheeks warmed a little at the thought, lips lifting in a faint smile. "It's not like either of you need to stay in Wallace." Oh, it broke my heart to say so, but if getting out of Vesterville House meant a chance for Thalia to come to terms with her depression, I'd put them on a plane myself.

"That sounds really amazing, actually." She straightened, kissed Belladonna on the forehead. "I'll mention it to Callie when she gets home tonight." She wrinkled her nose. "They're filming late, she said."

"Just don't tell her it was my idea," I said far too hastily, knowing I was giving my clandestine and unwelcome visit away. "Or that I was here?" I went for an exaggerated wince, so Calliope Thalia laughed before leaning in and hugging me with one arm, kissing my cheek with her cool lips. She felt cold, her whole body, chilled like this dreadful house and I caught myself hoping they would leave because honestly? If any place could actually carry a curse for reals?

Freaking Vesterville Creepy House could.

It was sunset by the time I left her, orange light just visible over the top of the towering house casting this end in that lovely blue light photographers seemed to adore. She seemed perkier, even came to the door to wave and smile after saying yes to dinner to which Lloyd seemed delighted. Which meant maybe my visit—okay, Belladonna's visit, let's be truthful here—made a difference after all.

Guilt still in evidence, however, I texted Calliope as I climbed behind the wheel. *I love you.* That was all. Hopefully, she'd take that love into consideration when she realized I'd been here (of course she'd figure it out) and was deciding if she was going to disown me or not.

I was just pulling into my driveway when Cherise messaged me. *Only one water bottle from Violet's room had Zexan in it*, she sent, *but good call on the delivery system. Looks like we have our source. We just need our suspect. I'm on my way to the hotel to pick up Emma Fontaine now. She might not have a script but it's too much of a coincidence for my liking.*

Well, crap, but I knew that she had to be thorough. Wait, the hotel? *She'll be on set*, I sent. *Aren't they filming tonight?*

Set's dark, according to Bronwyn Carpenter, Cherise sent.

Huh. So why did Calliope tell Thalia she'd be working a late shoot? Maybe she'd been mistaken? I was about to fire off another message to my kid to see what was up when she beat me to it.

HELP.

Calliope? What——? Oh no.

Please tell me I was the only woman in my family who put herself in harm's way because she was nosy. My tires squealed their concerns as I raced for the set and my best guess at finding my daughter before whatever her cry for assistance meant got the better of her.

Just look out if Violet's killer touched one hair on Calliope's head. There'd be another corpse joining the fallen star and it wouldn't be my daughter's.

CHAPTER EIGHTEEN

I fired off a text to Cherise as I pulled up to the gate, the young security guard letting me through right away, though my anxious questions about Calliope were met with bemused confusion.

He wasn't going to be any help.

Calliope's in trouble, I sent to the sheriff. *I'm at the film lot. Please help.* Then leaped out of the car and ran for the façade of a town before panting to a halt in the middle of the fraud, heart pounding, texting Calliope. *Where are you?* I probably should have thought to ask her that when the initial text came through, but I wasn't really thinking straight at that point. Nor was I going to be anytime soon. An, *On my way*, from Cherise had me feeling a little more confident but only having my kid in front of me, safe and sound, would end the nervous anxiety making my knees tremble and my pulse race.

For all I knew she wasn't even here. Maybe she'd been in a car accident and was on the side of the road. I'd leaped to a conclusion and could only hope that instinctive act didn't mean Calliope's present circumstances would lead to her harm because I hadn't thought things through.

Standing here waiting for her to text me back wasn't going to get me anywhere, that much was certain. I spun and ran for the back of the lot, deciding a search might at least turn up a hint or two as to where she was. Hoping, anyway, because hope was all I had to go on.

The place was dark, a few watch lights casting long shadows from the tall poles they'd been mounted on, the bright white actually making it harder to see, not easier. I jumped at a million nothings, stopping as I wove through the crowded back end of the film set, listening for a second or two before carrying on, my phone silent in my hand. Just my luck, I didn't spot a single security guard and now kicked myself I hadn't demanded the young man at the gate summon one to help me search. Thought and action had become disjointed and as I panic-panted my way past the dark and quiet craft services station and passed the workout space, I circled around to the line of trailers, the last place I had to look.

Checked doors, most of them locked, a few open but empty, the final one's door ajar. Violet's RV, now Darby's and the faintest motion as the trailer rocked slightly.

Someone was inside. Could it be Calliope? Or someone trying to hurt her? You'd think I'd have looked for some kind of weapon, right? I'm not sure if you've ever been in a situation where someone you truly love is threatened, if the kind of gnawing panic and near hysteria that comes with it has ever driven you to act in ways you normally wouldn't, without logic or foresight, pushed by pure adrenaline and instinct.

This was one of those moments, though I did have enough self-control remaining to creep into the RV rather than charge ahead like a savage bull on the attack. Momma Bear knew sneaking up on whoever it was crept through the trailer was a weapon in itself.

That meant as I took the second step, head whipping toward peripheral motion on my left, I caught sight of my prey, bending over an immobile shape collapsed on the sofa. Just enough light made it through the narrow windows I was able to make out the form lying there was a person, and that the rounded cheek and curls laying over it belonged to my kid.

The other person crouched next to her, hand reaching out. I'd had enough, stomped the last step and raced forward, as Emma Fontaine looked up in the dimness with her eyes huge and shining in the low light, expression clearly surprised at my arrival.

"Get away from her," I snarled. Emma backed off instantly, pressing herself against the counter behind her, while I stumbled to Calliope, checked her pulse, her breathing. Gasped out a sob of relief she seemed to be okay, though as I turned her head slightly, I noted the large, red welt on her temple, under her hair.

Someone struck her and knocked her unconscious. And that someone was standing right behind me.

I straightened and spun, fury overtaking terror. "She didn't do anything to you," I said. Okay, yelled. Loudly.

Emma flinched, nodded. "I know," she said. Looked down at my unconscious daughter in shock and her own fear. "I didn't hurt her, Dr. Pringle. I just found her like that."

"Right," I snapped back, anger taking me.

"Just like you didn't drug and kill Violet, right?" There was no proof and no prescription in her name and I was without any means to give strength to the case, but I knew it, *knew*. Concern for her, compassion aside, there was no doubt in my mind the young woman in front of me was responsible for everything.

Which meant my logical mind took a back seat while my emotions went to accusation and my voice agreed and my mouth let those words out without a fight.

She didn't argue. Didn't even try to deny it. Wait, you mean I was right?

Apparently so. Emma shuddered, tears trickling, shining lines down her face catching the bit of light through the window. "I never meant for Vi to die," she said, voice trembling. "I swear I didn't. I just…"

"You just wanted to hurt her," I said, throwing that in her face. "You just wanted her to *suffer*." My temper was in control and I refused to rein it in. "You ruined her, Emma, on purpose and then you killed her."

But Emma was shaking her head, not really in denial, more in defense. "You don't understand," she wailed.

"I understand enough." I backed off a bit, breathing heavily, firmly between her and

Calliope who was still out of it. If she thought I was letting her anywhere near my kid, she had another thing coming. Like, a solid punch in the face and a takedown of epic proportions that Hollywood would envy. "I understand she bullied you in high school before you transitioned." Emma nodded, sobbing softly. "I understand you blamed her for the death of your friend." More nodding, no attempt to interrupt. "I understand you set out to ruin Violet when you realized you were in a position to do so because she didn't know. Did she?" I slammed those words against Emma like blows and she flinched over and over from them. "She had no idea who you used to be, and she trusted you." My stomach churned, the entire mess making me sick. "She had no one to trust, Emma. She was lost and broken and hurting. She had her own story. And while she wasn't always a good person, she didn't deserve this."

Emma's sobbing slowed, quieted as she wiped at her face with both shaking hands. "I know." She sagged, her misery clear on her face, my eyes fully adjusted to the low light. "I hated her for a long time, you know. But when I transitioned and finally was happy with who I am... I forgot all about Violet." She was hugging herself now, shaking despite the support of the counter she leaned on. "I put her and our history behind us. All of my past. I was actually happy."

"So why go after her?" I was beginning to realize my conclusion jumping might have taken me off on the wrong path after all, but I wasn't willing to let go of my anger or protectiveness just yet. Because it wasn't just Calliope I was protecting at the moment. It was Violet, despite the fact she'd never need anyone to protect her again. "Why this vendetta?"

Emma looked away, licking her lips, and when she spoke again her voice was stronger if full of grief. "I didn't set out to hurt her," she said. "I was hired for a movie and she signed on last minute. I asked to be assigned to another actor, but she insisted and that was that. She didn't know who I was, you're right." Emma seemed softly in awe of that fact, turning her head, meeting my eyes with a little wonder there. "She adored me all of a sudden. Like I really was someone else. It felt great. For a while." Emma swallowed hard, shrugged. "But she hadn't lost her cruelty, her mean streak. And when she was horrible to one of the other artists, an openly gay man she taunted and tormented like it was funny, I snapped." More of my anger seeped out of me while hers mounted like we traded emotions in that tiny space. "I only wanted her to suffer a little," she said. "Everyone in town knew about her mother and her addiction to Zexan. I'd been prescribed it before I was transitioned, under my dead name." That was why Cherise didn't know she had the drugs. "I come from a small town. The local doctor still calls me male." She sounded disgusted by that. "The only upside? He was willing to write me scripts."

"In your dead name," I said.

She shrugged. "It was just meant to be a little thing." Right, because it certainly wasn't premeditated if she purposely possessed a prescription written for a person she wasn't anymore in order to punish someone she used to know. "I didn't expect..." she jerked slightly, as though confronting what she'd done gave her a physical reaction. "I justified it, slipping that pill into her water. That I'd only do it once. To be honest, I didn't even think it would do anything at all. But it worked." She shook her head, dark bob swinging, the blue in it just visible in the low light. "She lost her crap on set that day, way more aggressive and angrier than usual. And when she came down, she crashed hard." Emma caught her breath. "One pill," she said.

"It only took one pill and she had withdrawals." Her face twisted in clear misery. "I know I should have stopped, but I couldn't. Not at first. And then I couldn't because the reality was coming off them was worse than her on them." She'd settled into her guilt visibly, shaking stopped, resignation taking over. "I had to keep giving them to her," she said. "Or she would have crashed completely."

"You did stop," I said, calling her on that lie, "a few times. In between movies."

Emma's gaze flickered away, back to me, licking her lips again. "You're right," she said. "But every time I decided to stop, that this would be the last time... she asked for it." Emma tossed her bob, face now sullen, angry. "That's what she would say to us, you know. The kids she teased. If there wasn't anything wrong with us, she'd leave us alone." Her gaze had flattened out to rage. "We were asking for it."

I know I should have been on Emma's side, at least a little, but I couldn't condone what she'd done. Not knowing what horrors shaped Violet into the person she was. Both women deserved better and neither got it and that was the sad and wretched truth.

"Emma," I said, "I do understand. I get

it." My fury and protectiveness had faded back into the periphery, though I was still a human shield for my kid and, let's face it, always would be. "Violet had her own problems, though, and drugging her wasn't going to make them go away." Emma nodded the barest agreement. "Is that why you killed her?"

That earned me a firm headshake to the negative. "I drugged her," she said. "I tortured her for a year with those meds, knowing exactly what they were doing to her. But I swear to you, Dr. Pringle, I did *not* kill Violet." She had the good grace to flinch. "Not directly. I assumed she jumped, that the Zexan finally got to be too much." Emma hesitated. "I accidentally double-dosed her that day." There was the guilt, the barest breath of it returning. "But I was out for a run when she died. So, if someone killed her, it wasn't me." She started shaking again, tears resuming. "I wanted her to suffer. I wanted to ruin her for what she did. I never wanted her suffering to end." Jaw tight, poisoned truth laid bare, Emma shook her head one more time. "I never would have ended it, given a choice. Never."

That kind of hate would eat her up inside. But it wasn't my problem at the moment, because the trouble was, I believed her.

"What are you doing here?" If she didn't kill Violet, what was her reason for sneaking around in the dark?

"Darby texted me," she said. "Wanted me to meet her here."

"After dark, when the set's closed," I said. Let that sink in a minute while Emma's understanding evolved. "Someone knows what you've been up to." And that someone took advantage of Violet's state of mind. The killer.

"I found Calliope like this," Emma said then, faint panic rising in her voice. "I didn't want anyone else to get hurt. Is this my fault?"

I didn't answer that. "If you didn't push Violet over the balcony," I said, "who did?" Who hurt my daughter and who killed the young star? Because they were one and the same, no question.

"I did," Bronwyn Carpenter said, clearing the last step as both Emma and I turned with matching gasps to find the director at the door, gun leveled at both of us. "Now, if you'll be so kind, I need to make sure Emma goes away for murder."

CHAPTER NINETEEN

"*You* killed Violet?" Emma seemed floored by that. "She was your star. You needed her."

"I *needed*," Bronwyn snarled between clenched teeth, firm hand on the pistol she held showing no sign of hesitation or nervousness, "Violet Hyde to do her *job*. I didn't *need*," she jerked the muzzle in Emma's direction, "for the crazy woman you made her to ruin *everything*." She looked about ready to pull the trigger then and there but twitched as though fighting the urge to do so. "This was my last shot, you stupid girl," she snarled. "My last chance at redemption. I had to beg and pull in every favor I'd ever earned to even be considered for this job, and your selfishness means I'm never going to direct another movie ever again."

"You ruined your own reputation," Emma shot back. Right, of course. I'd become so fixated on the person drugging her I failed to realize there might be another reason someone would kill Violet. Case in point. "If you hadn't blown off the last two films, you'd still be employable."

"I'm well aware of my failings," Bronwyn shot back. "You think it's easy being a woman in Hollywood? A director? I'm not some hack makeup artist, girl. I'm in charge of the whole production." Bronwyn slapped her free hand against her thigh. "You have no idea the kind of pressure I'm talking about."

"I know you're an alcoholic," Emma shot back, as though the personal slight triggered her anger all over again, rebellion and hostility crossing her face. I actually held her back, that protectiveness I'd never lose for my daughter rising to engulf Emma now that a gun was in play and the killer exposed. "And a drug addict and no one wants to work with you because you flake out when you're needed."

"I've made mistakes," Bronwyn said, without a shred of apology in her tone or her stance. "But I put the work in, and I got clean." She shook her head, jaw jumping as she clenched and unclenched, while I worried Emma might be prodding her too much for all our sakes. "Violet was going to be my relaunch, my big chance to prove I'd changed. I had it all laid out, exactly the way it was supposed to go. And then you decide your feelings are hurt and you ruined this for everyone."

Emma couldn't argue that truth. "I'm not sorry," she whispered. Then looked startled as if she didn't realize she'd said it out loud. "I'm not," she repeated, stronger this time, her old hate and determined rage returning.

"I know," Bronwyn said. "That's why you're the perfect person to set up for her murder." She sighed then, gesturing at me, at Calliope. "You two weren't supposed to get involved," she said. "This could have ended neat and tidy. But now you're part of the problem. I'll deal with all three of you, but believe me, I don't like doing it."

She had no idea Cherise was on the way. I just had to keep her talking, keep her distracted.

"How ever did you find out Emma was drugging Violet?" Seemed a logical question to fill the gap between my mind's scramble to find a way to hold out a little longer and its panic we were going to die and there was nothing I could do to stop Bronwyn from shooting us.

"I knew the signs," Bronwyn said. "Had a grip who reacted the same way to Zexan. He had a heck of a time with withdrawal, so I knew it had to be something similar. The aggression, the unexplained anger. Violet was always volatile, but not like that. And it was so much worse this past year. I almost chose someone else." She grunted, rubbed her face with her free hand. "Why didn't I just go with another actress? But I didn't and as soon as I realized she was taking the drug I confronted her about it."

"And she denied it," I said.

"Adamantly," Bronwyn said. "Furiously. Which meant there was only one way she could have been taking it." She gestured at Emma. "I looked into you when I realized you were the only one close enough to her and who she trusted. Easy enough to find that blog of yours, who you used to be, who she was to you." The same truths I'd uncovered. Why did I feel like I was two steps behind? Because I was. "Once I put it together, I realized I had to get her clean or the film would be shot." She didn't realize the irony of that word, apparently, my brain's logical and pattern recognizing functions doing its job despite the tense situation. "I went to talk to her. Just talk." She fell silent then, gaze far away. She had to have been reliving the night of Violet's death and I could only imagine how it unfolded. Then didn't have to imagine, because Bronwyn went on, voice as distant as her attention. "She was a mess, worse than I'd ever seen her."

"I gave her a double dose," Emma said, repeating what she'd told me. "I didn't mean to." I wasn't sure I believed that anymore, not after everything she'd said, her admission of continuing guilt.

Bronwyn didn't seem to appreciate Emma's honesty. "You fool," she snarled then. "She was practically incoherent, running on about the cast and crew and her mother and how she hated everyone. She was violent, in the end." Bronwyn's face flickered at last, the resolute anger cracking, showing horror through the edges. So, she did regret what happened? "I followed her out to the balcony. She was leaning over it, babbling on and on and I just couldn't take it. I grabbed her, tried to pull her back inside. She turned on me, like an animal." Bronwyn swallowed, hard, twice. Her lips trembled before she spoke again, the effort appearing to take almost more than she had to give. "She tried to claw me, kicked me. She was wearing the shoes." The shoes? Right, those costume shoes she obsessed over that night. Bronwyn mentioned them at the scene, wanted them back. Because they were evidence she killed Violet?

Of course. The chlorinated DNA on the outside of the sparkly red stilettos.

Bronwyn went on. "She tried to hit me, and I pushed her." She flinched from that moment, came back from the past to catch her breath and settle once again into harsh reality. "She fell. I grabbed for her, caught one of the shoes. Scraped my hand." She looked down at her free one. "I knew if they tested the sequins, they'd find my DNA. And I'm in the system."

"That's why you wanted the shoes back," I said.

Bronwyn glared at me. "I could only hope the water destroyed the evidence."

"It did," I said. "The chlorine did."

She nodded. "Sometimes this job and the things you learn make hiding what happened easier."

Made sick sense. Though I didn't ask her which show she'd worked on that offered her that comfort. She fell silent a moment, gone into the past again, it seemed, though the gun never wavered.

"Bronwyn," I said, very softly so as not to antagonize her as Emma had been doing. Her gaze snapped to me. "You could have saved her. Why didn't you save Violet?"

"I thought she'd get out of the pool on her own," she said, the faintest wail of protest in her words, just hovering in the back of her voice, as though a giant scream had been forced to merely whisper. "I didn't know she passed out. I would have saved her. But I knew she'd accuse me. I didn't know what to do." Again that hand tossed and slapped her thigh, everything about her so suddenly accusatory, blaming. "I panicked, all right? I panicked and ran and figured I'd be fired or arrested. Not that Violet would be found drowned." She shook her head, one final slap of her leg loud in the quiet after her outburst. "I swear, I didn't know she was dead." She stiffened then, waved the gun at us. "It's too late now, anyway. I'm done, my career is over. But I'm not going to prison for murder." She took a step back away from the stairs further down the right side of the trailer. "We're all going to take a walk now," she said. "And I'm going to make sure the real killer, the one who set Violet up for this, goes down for her death."

CHAPTER TWENTY

Emma wavered next to me, and I knew she was ready to obey Bronwyn's order, though out of her guilt and need to pay for what she'd done or just a simple ingrained habit of following the direction of her superiors I wasn't sure. Either way, going with Bronwyn meant only one thing and I wasn't about to just let the three of us walk like sheep into a slaughterhouse.

It was in that moment she held Bronwyn's attention with her decided compliance I realized Calliope was awake. My daughter's eyes opened, her head turned away from the door, concealing her state from our captor but granting me enough relief I almost gave her away.

"My daughter didn't do anything," I said

then, blurting anything I could to keep
Bronwyn talking. Any second now Cherise
was going to come through that door. Any
second now. Like *now*, Cherise. Come on, it
was a fifteen-minute drive from the sheriff's
office to the lot. What was taking her so long?

Every second I was positive she'd appear.
Except she didn't and I kept babbling because
surely rescue was right there.

Right.

There.

Crappy.

"Your daughter asks too many questions,"
Bronwyn said. "I heard her asking about
Emma and her friend, realized your clever
little PA kid figured out what Emma had been
up to."

"Problem solved," I said. "You could have
just let Emma take the fall."

Bronwyn's head shook side to side, her
expression grim. "I had to act before anyone
could question our drug dealer here about
Violet's death. Sure, they might not have
believed her when she said she didn't do it,
but I had to be positive she couldn't deny it."
She let out a long and angry breath. "This is
pointless. It's time to end this. You," she
jabbed the gun at Emma, "are going to sign
the confession letter I wrote, all about the

fight you had with Violet, how you hated her, how you drugged her and then pushed her over the balcony. And how these two," my turn to have the gun pointed at me, then Calliope while my Momma Bear growled her threat, "figured it out and you killed them, too, before offing yourself."

Honestly? It was the kind of plan that likely would have worked. Without any reason to suspect Bronwyn, DNA evidence washed away in the pool, the only person with any motive and connection to Violet's state and end was Emma. And it was very plausible—Cherise knew me too well—that I'd have figured out what I already had figured out and come here to confront the makeup artist. The internet search on my computer at home would bear out my discovery, as would my warning to Cherise about Emma. And since Calliope was a chip off the old Pringle rock, the fact she, too, figured things out wasn't a stretch.

If the sheriff didn't show before Bronwyn shot us? She was going to get away with it, wasn't she?

"Now," Bronwyn snapped. "I'm done talking. Let's go."

Emma went without resistance, moving past me toward the door, her hands clutched to her chest, her head down. Resigned to her fate, apparently, while I was as far from that as I could get. I bent next to Calliope, pretending she was still unconscious.

"You hit her too hard," I snapped. "She won't wake up." If I could lure her closer, could I get the gun? Those were the types of terrible ideas that flashed into life in times like these, despite the fact wrestling for the weapon over my daughter's prone body increased the likelihood one or both of us would end up shot.

Bronwyn didn't risk it. "Pick her up," she said. "Carry her if you have to. Or I shoot her right here and now."

I did my best to keep Callie's cover, not sure if her playing at out of it was helping us or hindering, though the longer she stayed at it, the better. I did note, as I lifted her up into a ragdoll sitting position, she held a phone in her hands.

The screen flickered to life as a text came through. From Cherise.

My daughter had been busy.

The trouble was, Bronwyn caught the light, lunging forward and sticking the gun in my face, her rage a snarl of fury.

"What have you done?" She pulled her arm back to strike Calliope again. I stood abruptly, putting myself between her and my daughter, fearless in the moment.

"You touch her again," I said, "and I'll shoot you myself."

If Bronwyn believed me, she made no sign of it, though she did back up, head swiveling to check for Emma. I almost tsked at the makeup artist in frustration. She hadn't moved a muscle, rocking a little as she hugged herself and waited for Bronwyn. Definitely lost in her own time and place and deep in the regret of what she'd done or, at the very least, acceptance and willingness to take the kind of responsibility that ended in death.

We'd just see about that.

I helped Calliope to the stairs and down to the ground, the temptation to bolt cut short as Bronwyn leaped the last two steps and landed with the gun poised and ready.

"That way," she snapped. "And hurry."

"What did you tell Cherise?" I whispered that, hoping Calliope had managed to warn the sheriff about Bronwyn but instead of responding with words, my kid met my eyes and shook her head, her gaze full of fear.

No such luck. Clearly, she'd gotten something out, but the details had to be thin enough my kid knew Bronwyn was still in a position to get away with this if we didn't do something.

An endless stream of somethings then passed through my mind as we marched across the lot to the set, the pretty little park in the middle of the fake town and the fountain where Bronwyn had us stop. Pulled out a sheet of paper, folded in three. Handed it to Emma along with a pen.

The makeup artist turned without a word, face almost serene, and sat on the edge of the fountain. It was off for the night, the silent, black water-like glass, reflecting her face as she quickly signed the page.

"Put it in your pocket," Bronwyn said.

Emma folded it carefully back along the original lines before doing so one more time, in half, tears splashing down on the page as she did. Perfect, really, the final nail in the coffin of her guilt, and all the proof Cherise would need that the letter and the confession were real.

I had to do something. But what?

Emma tucked the page into her front jeans pocket, looking up at Bronwyn fearlessly, a deep sigh escaping her. "Now what? Are you going to shoot me first?" She reached out one hand, let it fall. "Please, shoot me first."

Bronwyn seemed shocked by the makeup artist's attitude. So much so, she hesitated.

And, knowing it was logically the worst possible choice but no longer able to hold myself back, I lunged.

For Bronwyn and the gun, right after placing both hands on my daughter's arm and shoving her as hard as I could.

I heard Calliope cry out, the thud as she hit the ground. As safe as I could make her, the best I could do and probably not enough but all I had in me. That, and this growling, snarling, furious Momma Bear who would not, under any circumstances, allow her daughter to die as long as there was breath in my body.

Emma's huge green eyes stared at me, that gaping shocked O returned as her full lips rounded in what almost seemed a silent scream while time slowed and I hovered in mid-leap, Bronwyn turning toward me, the gun rising, her fury returned in a flash of disappointment mixed with pain and near total disillusionment while I quickly closed the distance—oh, so freaking slowly, it seemed—my hands outstretched for her, entire body leaving the ground as I tackled her.

My hands connected with her body, my own crashing into her chest. Time returned to normal as I collapsed on top of her, someone shouting my name from the distance. Cherise, it had to be Cherise to the rescue, even as Calliope screamed.

And the gun.

Went off.

CHAPTER TWENTY-ONE

I winced as the bandage on my outer thigh rubbed against my shorts. Wouldn't you know, getting shot hurts, though honestly, I'd been lucky to get away with a flesh wound, but you wouldn't know it from the amount of complaining (and bleeding) I did when the EMTs patched me up.

If I never got shot again (please, no more shooting at me, thank you), it would be far too soon for my liking.

A gin and cranberry in hand as the perfect painkiller, I carried on with cooking dinner, anticipating the arrival of my guests any second. Belladonna perched on the counter, enjoying her tuna juice treat while I paused to pet her and kiss the top of her soft head.

The other thing about getting shot? You

learn to appreciate the fact small things matter more than big things and life was worth living the way you wanted.

Not that I didn't believe so in the first place, but my mortality brush was the closest I'd come to knowing what lay on the other side of that barrier to the next life and I was happy to embrace said appreciation if it kept me from going upstairs and curling up in bed to cry like a baby and never, ever leave the house ever again.

Oh, I thought about it, you betcha. Just as soon as I was sure my kid was okay.

Hard not to flashback to two nights ago, to Cherise arriving with three deputies and what seemed like an army of security, handcuffs snapping while Calliope collapsed next to me and hugged me, Bronwyn dragged away.

It had hurt, to have to tell Cherise what Emma had done. To watch the sheriff cuff the makeup artist as well. Made worse because Emma paused with a soft smile on her face.

"I was asking for it," she said.

Made me cry. Hardly surprising.

I felt my phone buzz, bringing me back to the present, looked down at the screen, dismissed the text from Trent. Yes, I knew he was worried but no, he didn't get to message me three million times in two days. I wasn't sure how many times I could reassure him I was fine or that he didn't get to badger me about it any longer.

My short talk with Richard last night had its bumps and bruises, too. While I knew his point for calling was to apologize, I hadn't meant to chastise him for his lack of assistance for Violet and, ultimately, when we both hung up it was with words spoken on both sides I for one (and hopefully he agreed) wished I could take back, even if they were true.

Sad to end a friendship on such a note, but seriously.

The front door opened after a single knock, Calliope calling out to me. I turned with a smile and a salute with my glass, hugging my kid when she came into the kitchen, then Thalia who smiled back at me, softly, shyly, but seemed more herself when she embraced me.

No time to ask her if she'd broached the travel topic with Calliope, at least without outing my involvement, because the rest of my guests were on their heels, Layla chattering happily with Calliope about the set while Cherise settled, hug acquired from everyone, at the counter while I poured her a drink and the three young women retreated to the living room with Belladonna to maul her before dinner.

"How's the leg?" My sheriff friend hadn't given me too hard of a time about getting shot, at least, though she'd been stiffly angry with me when we'd talked at the ambulance. Only to hug me and cry a few tears and admit she was terrified and if I ever did that again they'd never find my body.

Until I told her it was for Calliope. Which made her cry harder.

Being a mom had its challenges and I guess getting shot was one of them when you were Persephone Pringle.

I handed her a glass of my favorite concoction, saving her red wine for the roast I was about to serve. "Hurts," I said, leaning into the counter with the other leg.

"How're the nightmares?" She arched one perfect brow at me over the rim of her glass.

"Tolerable," I said. Even as memories of Calliope crying, Thalia, Emma, too and even Violet, but as babies, not grown women, haunted me, reminding me the influence of this case would be with me for a long time. Shrugged. "If I let myself freak out, I'll lose it, Cherise. This was a close one."

She offered up her glass and we clinked.

"You sure you want to make this official?" I'd been presented just this morning with a request from town council to make my consulting with the sheriff's department permanent, including—are you kidding me?— a badge. No gun, just something to flash at suspects, but it had an oddly satisfying feeling to it I couldn't turn down.

Besides, this seemed to be my thing now. How could I say no?

The girls emerged from the living room, Thalia holding Belladonna, Layla happily helping me serve as dinner unfolded. I finally took a seat, Cherise pouring herself a glass of wine, offering some to Thalia who, to my surprise, nodded to the affirmative. She rarely drank that I knew of, though she seemed to enjoy it when she sampled the vintage the sheriff brought.

"Now that the film's packing up and moving on," Cherise said, "are we losing you to Hollywood, Callie?" With the loss of their director, the producers informed town council they had no choice but to cut costs and strike the set. Not that I was all that upset about it, though the revenue lost was an unfortunate by-product. Still, it was summer and tourist trade was up, so the inconvenience of the extra occupants vacating wasn't as big a blow as it could have been.

Cherise's teasing had my daughter toss out her customary sigh and eye-roll.

"No chance," she said, squeezing Thalia's hand. "I'm done with the movies. Those people are *crazy*."

Tell me about it. From what I'd heard, Thomas Parker was now repping Darby Buell as his headliner. That took the final shreds of respect I may have managed and burned them to dust. As for Kole Ross, the rumor mill said he agreed to stay on with the movie while it was revamped, though I was sure he'd rather have just moved on.

Made me think about Emma. How she had tried to move on, and fate decided otherwise. She'd been arraigned, though her plea of not guilty due to insanity wasn't going to hold up in court. I wished her well, understood so clearly her motivation, but would never, ever be able to reconcile what she'd done to the woman I'd barely known and wished even now I could have helped.

Didn't stop me from worrying about the makeup artist. Being trans was hard enough. Being trans in the prison system was another thing entirely. Cherise assured me the prosecutor took that into consideration and hopefully they could work out some kind of deal that kept her safe. But the truth was, she'd done everything she could to ruin another person's life and career and, ultimately, was an accessory to her murder.

That kind of crime had to be paid for.

I could feel empathy for Bronwyn, as well, considering her circumstances. I had every confidence she hadn't set out to kill Violet, that it had been an accident, manslaughter at the most. Too much rode on Bronwyn's comeback. And yet, again, a young woman's life and career had been cut short because of old hurts, of addictions and a culture of celebrity that didn't allow for anything but perfection.

Violet's death had to have consequences to more than just Violet.

"Besides," Calliope said, teasing tone flipped to her. "I hear they're planning a true-crime biopic about Violet Hyde. And guess who's the lead character?"

I looked up from my drink to the silence that followed, caught a handful of wicked smiles aimed in my direction. Gaped as I realized the implications of that.

Laughed while they laughed with me.

"I wonder who they'll get to play Bella," I said.

Looking for more from Persephone Pringle? You're in luck! Book six, *Estate of Despairs*, is available right now!

ABOUT THE AUTHOR

Everything you need to know about me is in this one statement: I've wanted to be a writer since I was a little girl, and now I'm doing it. How cool is that, being able to follow your dream and make it reality? I've tried everything from university to college, graduating the second with a journalism diploma (I sucked at telling real stories), am an enthusiastic member of an all-girl improv troupe (if you've never tried it, I highly recommend making things up as you go along as often as possible) and I get to teach and perform with an amazing group of women I adore. I've even been in a Celtic girl band (some of our stuff is on YouTube!) and was an independent filmmaker. You can check out the whole Lovely Witches Club series for free at:

https://lovelywitchesclub.com.

My life has been one creative thing after another—all leading me here, to writing books for a living.

Now with multiple series in happy publication, I live on beautiful and magical Prince Edward Island (I know you've heard of Anne of Green Gables) with my multitude of pets.

I love-love-love hearing from you! You can reach me (and I promise I'll message back) at https://patti@pattilarsen.com/home. And if you're eager for your next dose of Patti Larsen books (usually about one release a month) come join my mailing list! All the best up and coming, giveaways, contests and, of course, my observations on the world (aren't you just dying to know what I think about everything?) all in one place:

https://bit.ly/PattiLarsenEmail.
Last—but not least!—I hope you enjoyed what you read! Your happiness is my happiness. And I'd love to hear just what you thought. A review where you found this book would mean the world to me—reviews feed writers more than you will ever know. So, loved it (or not so much), your honest review would make my day. Thank you!